Christmas Frontier Brides

A Mail Order Bride Holiday Collection

Hope Meadow Publishing

CHRISTMAS FRONTIER BRIDES

This book is a work of fiction. Names, characters, businesses, organizations, places, events and incidents either are the product of the author's imagination or are used fictitiously. Any resemblance to actual persons, living or dead, events, or locales is entirely coincidental.

ISBN-13: 978-1519693976
ISBN-10: 1519693974

First Edition: December 2015

CONTENTS

OLIVIA'S CHRISTMAS ON THE FRONTIER

Boston, 1856

"I swear, if that woman knits one more pair of mismatched slippers, we're going to have to start storing them in the stove!" Olivia fumed silently, stuffing the latest pair in the home's overflowing chest of drawers. The slippers themselves didn't really bother her so much, it was really the lecture that came with her aunt's completion of every pair that vexed her.

"You see, Olivia?" her aunt Margaret would say each time, holding up the ridiculous looking pair. "You could be making much better use of your time putting your hands to good work instead of taxing your brain with all of that learning. What in the world is a woman going to do with all that knowledge. Just a waste of time if you ask me," she'd finish.

While Olivia couldn't remember ever asking for her aunt's opinion, she'd just smile politely and nod. "Even if all that learning is wasted, at least it isn't overflowing the Hepplewhite," she'd muse silently.

She really was grateful to her aunt, it was just that they were such different people. Her parents used to send her to visit each year from the time Olivia was eleven years old, keeping her aunt company after uncle William passed away. During the last of those visits, her parents and younger brother fell terribly ill, taken to a special hospital before Olivia could return home. By the time she got back, not one of them remained. Tuberculosis had claimed each of their lives, leaving Olivia entirely alone at the young age of sixteen. Aunt Margaret had hurried to fetch her and she'd lived in her aunt's home ever since. If it weren't for the ornery, old-fashioned woman, Olivia couldn't imagine what fate would have befallen her.

Her aunt meant well, always trying to prepare Olivia in the areas that she felt would make her niece a better wife someday. The only thing aunt

Margaret spent more time doing than knitting these past five years together was primping and priming Olivia for every outing, instructing her in cooking and housekeeping, and lecturing her on all the things that made up a proper lady. But Olivia didn't have any interest in becoming a good and proper wife. In fact, she had actively resisted the courting of a multitude of young men—and a few old—since she'd come to live in Boston.

Olivia wanted more out of life than her aunt's limited vision; she wanted to learn everything her mind could absorb, travel to new places, meet people from all over the world—or at least from somewhere outside of New England. She wanted it so much that she could feel restlessness in her veins at any given moment of the day. All she could do was read about the ventures of others in her books and pray for the day she might experience even a modicum of the excitement had by explorers like Lewis and Clark, Sacajewea, Ida Pfeiffer and James Weddell.

With that hope fresh in her mind, Olivia sat down at the wobbly wooden table in the kitchen, opening the daily paper. She read it nearly cover to cover most days, even when the most exciting news was local events and coffee advertisements. There was only one section of the entire paper she skipped over on a regular basis, but for some unknown reason it drew her attention today. Perhaps it was the lack of intriguing or exciting news combined with a renewed surge of restlessness coursing through her, or maybe she'd taken leave of her senses. She'd never entertained the prospect of marriage before but as she browsed through the advertisements of men out west looking for wives from the east, she didn't immediately dismiss the notion.

She never had any intention in marrying; the institution seemed to carry only the prospect of squelching her dreams. She'd seen it happen. Young girls so full of excitement and curiosity at the start of adulthood, but once wed, it appeared to strip that from them, leaving them content to tidy a house and chase after youngsters, seldom even venturing beyond the walls of their homes. Instead, Olivia was stuck within the confines of her aunt's home, seldom venturing any further than the local market. She was intrigued by the fact that these men in the newspaper advertisements were offering not only adventure, but a brand new life in a foreign place.

As she skimmed through the page of advertisements, Olivia felt less hopeful by the moment. It seemed a wife wasn't the only thing some of these men were after; one required a woman with at least $20,000, another wanted a mild-mannered woman well-versed in keeping house. Some were fifty-year-old men seeking eighteen-year-old brides, and Olivia did her best not to bristle at the thought of being forever tied to a rough, old man with a proclivity for young girls. As she scanned through the page, it was easy to read between the lines; there were plenty of men looking for pretty ladies to wash their laundry and cook their meals.

"I can stay here with Aunt Margaret and do all that just fine, thank you," Olivia whispered aloud, coming to the conclusion that she'd been right thus far in skipping over the silly section of the newspaper. Just as she was about to toss the newspaper aside an advertisement right there in the middle of the page caught her attention. She must have overlooked it somehow, or perhaps fate had been saving the best for last.

"A man of thirty five in search of an intelligent, adventurous young woman to build a life together in California," it read.

"Now that's something you don't read about every day," she thought.

She hadn't really given the idea much consideration, reading through the advertisements more out of curiosity than with any serious intent. But, staring down at the man's ad now, she couldn't help but contemplate the possibility. Her life here was so monotonous with no real chance of her circumstances changing anytime in the near future. If she wanted a change, perhaps she had to be the one to make it happen. And if this man was looking for a woman with a sense of adventure, he certainly couldn't be counted in with the same boring, humdrum collection of men she'd happened upon during her time in Boston with Aunt Margaret. All she had to do to open up the opportunity for a new life was to write a letter to him. She didn't have to commit herself to marriage this moment. She'd consider a more concrete decision if and when the man from California sent a response.

Olivia rose to fetch a pen and paper and quickly started to scrawl before she could change her mind. She had absolutely no idea what people usually wrote in these types of letters, but figured that an introduction and a little about herself was a reasonable guess.

Dear Sir,

I would like to introduce myself. My name is Olivia Collins. I have lived with my aunt in Boston, Massachusetts for the past several years, prior to which I resided with my mother and father, and younger brother in Ashfield. My father owned a factory and my mother, I am not ashamed to admit, spent a great deal of her time helping him in his business dealings.

While I was never formally schooled, my parents possessed a deep passion for learning, teaching my brother and I both to read and write from a young age. I inherited their passion it appears, and cannot ever seem to obtain enough knowledge. Subjects as varied as science and medicine to philosophy and history fascinate me beyond words. However, I must admit a particular fondness for the tales of new adventurers and explorers like Nicholas Baudin, Allan Cunningham and Hester Stanhope.

I feel it only fair to tell you that prior to today I had not previously considered finding a companion in such a manner. I do hope you understand that it is not an unappealing prospect, but rather not the ordinary means of going about making a marriage. Upon seeing your advertisement, the possibility of life and adventure in a new place held an immense amount of appeal. I have read a little about those brave souls who have ventured out west in search of better lives for themselves and for their families back home. I would be excited to learn about your own experience, if it is not too forward of me to say.

It is my hope that I might receive your response, so that we may have the opportunity to get to know one another.

Sincerely,

Olivia Collins

She considered briefly as she wrote if she should mention her age, or extol her physical attributes, but if the man was really only interested in a young beauty, Olivia was afraid he would have to find one elsewhere. She slipped the letter into an envelope and headed out quickly, sending it off before she could reconsider. While she hadn't given the idea of marriage—or moving across the country to California—a single thought prior to that day, she found it invaded her thoughts almost constantly from the moment her letter began making its way to the unknown man across the country. At first, she wondered if she had acted too hastily, but as the days and weeks passed, Olivia found herself awaiting a response with increasing anxiousness. She read about the farmers and miners who had begun moving to the west in search of a better life. Land was free or cheap and there was plenty of it to be had. They were adventurers, in her opinion, willing to sacrifice comfort and consistency in their old lives in search of the unknown. The idea sent a thrill coursing through Olivia's body, and already she had developed a modicum of respect for the man in the advertisement. "He must be brave, or at the very least, determined," she thought, and either one of those characteristics was a positive in her mind.

She wondered what else there was to be discovered about him. Did he have family there with him or had he ventured across the country on his own? Was he an educated man or did he give his life to mining or farming because there were no other occupations in which his limited intelligence would enable him to succeed. In truth, she also wondered other things about him, though she'd never confess those curiosities aloud, like whether he was a handsome man, made strong by the work that occupied his time. Or was he ugly and plump? Not that it mattered much; Olivia didn't think a good match required attractive faces and desirous bodies.

It was just such thinking that had her fending off the attention of young men there in Boston—men who knew nothing about her but for her physical attributes, and on that basis alone were convinced she'd be a fitting wife. Olivia was certainly a beauty—she wasn't so modest that she would deny it, but she wasn't the least bit impressed by a man who would use her long, auburn hair, chestnut eyes, soft, feminine features or her slim form as a gauge of her lifelong compatibility.

She forced the matter of marriage from her mind then. It was early in the morning and she wasn't going to spend the entire day obsessing over the man from California nor how he would choose a wife. In the midst of clearing the table after breakfast, Olivia turned her attention to the tasks at hand, washing the dishes and the wobbly table, before readying herself for the day's errands. While her aunt's maid was responsible for the daily upkeep of the home, she didn't see any harm in helping out with the chores around the house; it was an awful lot of work for one woman to manage.

Then Olivia was off, choosing to walk the short distance between stops rather than bother with her aunt's horse and carriage. There was a stop to make at the market, a book to return to the library on Mason Street and a trip to the post office to squeeze into the morning hours.

****

Olivia had been ecstatic when the library opened to the public in March of 1854. She had spent countless hours in the reading room, absorbing knowledge from so many more books than her aunt's bookshelves could hold. Later, when books from the library began to circulate, the building became a regular stop on her travels, and until recently, the most exciting point of any outing. The past several days, she'd saved the post office for last on her list, entering with bated breath as she asked about mail for herself or her aunt. On the second day, a letter had indeed arrived, but it had been addressed to her aunt from an acquaintance in a nearby town. She smiled graciously at the clerk, but inside she felt an enormous sense of disappointment. She hadn't realized she'd been anxiously awaiting the California man's response until that moment, but it seemed with each passing day, the idea had grown on her a little more to the point that she was now quite certain she had made the right call in sending the letter.

As she entered the post office after making the other necessary stops along her way, she did her best to remain calm. There was absolutely no guarantee the man would respond to her letter at all, and so there was no reason for the anticipation she could feel welling within her. She felt her breath catch in her throat as the clerk left to search for her mail—a response she was regrettably becoming accustomed to after too many trips to the post office in recent days. As the clerk returned with a letter in hand, the anticipation she'd tried to keep in check coursed through her.

"There is one for you today, Miss," the clerk smiled at her kindly.

"Thank you very much," Olivia replied, doing her best to feign a visage of nonchalance.

But as she turned away and walked out of the post office, she read her name and address over and over again, handwritten neatly on the front of the envelope. There was nobody else who would be sending her letters—she hadn't received a single correspondence from her few acquaintances back in Ashfield in several years. The letter had to be from the man in California. She continued walking toward home, the letter clenched in her hand all the while. She wanted to indecorously rip it open right there in the street like it were gold contained within the envelope rather than a letter. She hurried home instead, refusing to give into the curiosity that plagued her. If her feet wanted to propel her there faster, who was she to refuse?

Not twenty minutes later, Olivia walked through the front door of her Aunt Margaret's house and deposited her new book from the library along with her purchases from the market on the wobbly kitchen table. Seeing her aunt engrossed in her knitting, she sat down, placing the envelope in front of her and with the most composure she could muster, opened the letter.

"Dear Miss Collins," the same neat handwriting from the envelope

penned the greeting.

It was a pleasure to receive your letter. Please allow me to introduce myself. My name is Jackson King and I am originally from Cambridge, Massachusetts. I traveled to San Francisco, California nearly five years ago in search of a new and different life from a rather mundane existence in New England. The west has been replete with challenges and it is certainly not for the lackadaisical or weak, but it is certainly unlike any experience that could be had back east; a land not yet refined or corrupted by polite society, and ready to be wrought in any form or shape a pair of dedicated hands may desire.

I have thoroughly enjoyed the adventure. While the first year here presented a substantial amount of solitude to which I was unaccustomed, I am the eldest of five brothers, all of whom have since joined me here in San Francisco, California. The youngest of my brothers, William, only recently joined us. In fact, he arrived just in time to celebrate the last Christmas holiday. Though our celebrations may not be as elaborate as they were in Cambridge, we enjoyed a plethora of good food, song, and the best company to be found in the east or west. Until they came here, I had not fully realized how much I had enjoyed our time together and their arrival brought along new additions to our family as three of my brothers have married, and two have presented me with nieces and nephews. I admit to playing a part in making those youngsters some of the most spoiled children in the state of California, perhaps in the entire country.

I was pleased to read about your fondness for learning. Having attended college prior to moving out west, I share with you an undying interest in acquiring knowledge. While it was an unnecessary venture for a man determined to mine his fortune with his hands, it was an enriching experience nevertheless that served only to bolster an unquenchable thirst for intellectual growth. One of my favorite rooms in my home is the library. It has been filled with a multitude of books hand-picked by myself...until recently, as it seems there is a mounting number of children's fables gracing the shelves.

I do hope you will write again soon.

Sincerely,

Jackson King

While Olivia wasn't generally the type to sum up a person so quickly, she couldn't help but to feel an immediate affinity to Jackson King. He was intelligent and adventurous, and yet it was evident from the fondness with which he spoke about his family, there was a deeper and kinder side to him as well. It was surely too early to conclude anything with any certainty, but she was inclined to believe this was a man with whom she would be content.

A love match? She wouldn't speculate on such a silly thing. Olivia had never seen love abounding within any marriage and was prone to believe "true love" was nothing more than a myth. Perhaps more aptly, a story told to children by mothers with good intentions, but who do little more than concoct unreasonable expectations in impressionable, young minds. When she considered the possibility of marriage to the man from California, Olivia thought of the potential for lively, intelligent discussion with Mr. King. A man with an eagerness for knowledge and adventure; surely their conversations would never be dull and that was enough for Olivia—to find a man who would value her opinions and intellect, who would not judge her to be daft or stupid solely on the basis of her being a woman. She could live in harmony with such a man. So, without hesitation this time, Olivia pulled out pen and paper and immediately began her reply, feeling surprisingly comfortable conversing with the California man.

Dear Mr. King,

I enjoyed receiving your letter and I was pleased to read about our shared enthusiasm for intellectual pursuits. I smiled as I read about your family. I imagine it was heartwarming to have those you care about so close as you began your new life out west. I wish I could relate to such a circumstance now, but I am afraid I have very little family to speak of, having lost both my parents and young brother to tuberculosis when I was only sixteen. I can recall a multitude of fond memories made with each of them and I treasure those dearly. How I long for a family celebration like those you spoke of in your letter. It is only my aunt and myself here in Boston, and our quiet, little Holidays together pale in comparison to the notion of a grand family event. I think that would be exciting to have small children around the house, though I cannot profess any personal experience in such matters. My brother and I were close in age, and there have been no other youngsters around but for the few I greet at the market.

I have read a great deal about California in the past several weeks, and I must tell you that it sounds tremendously exciting. Perhaps I should say that I want to tame the west like so many others in polite society in New England seem to feel prudent, but I confess, I would not change it one bit.

Perhaps that is not entirely true. I read that the weather there is terribly warm, particularly in comparison to the cold and snowy winters in New England and it is precisely that snow I would bring with me there if I could. I cannot imagine a Christmas with the streets bare and the grass green. It is nearly as inconceivable as one's own mortality, is it not? Though I think it would be quite amusing to adorn an Oleander or Indian Laurel tree in the parlor.

I will look forward to receiving your response.

Warm regards,

Olivia Collins

Olivia sent the letter off without a second thought, already anxious to receive a reply but knowing it would be several weeks at least. She allowed her mind to wander as she walked the few short blocks back to her aunt's home, thinking about how her life would be different if she moved away and married a stranger that she had never met. From the second she found

Mr. King's advertisement in the newspaper until she handed over the letter at the post office just a few moments ago, she had been indecisive, not entirely certain this was the path for her, but at some point during the brief stroll home, Olivia came to a decision. This was it. There would be no more debate, no more questioning or vacillating. Barring some strange or unpredictable event, she was prepared to accept the proposal insinuated in Mr. King's advertisement. She longed for a new and different life, a conversation with someone who knew something more than the finest wool to use for knitting or the proper way to arrange the dinner table. She wanted to know if it really was as warm in California as the stories she'd heard. Was it really a lawless place with nary a woman in sight for miles? Was the land really teeming with gold, and what did a palm tree look like up close?

She stopped mid-step as she affirmed her decision silently, changing directions in search of the library instead. If she was going to travel to some foreign place, if California was truly going to become her home, Olivia wanted to know everything. Walking through the library's front door, Olivia got to work. She investigated what was involved in gold mining out west, learning about those who had been successful thus far and in what ways she might be able to contribute when she arrived in California. She researched what methods of transportation were available from New England to the west and how daily living differed between the two places. Long before she was finished, the sun began to set in the sky, reminding Olivia she should be hurrying home. Besides, her head felt so full, she couldn't imagine where her brain had stored so much information.

****

The next day, she slipped away to the library after her morning chores to investigate further. "It is as worthwhile a way to pass the time as any," she reasoned, diving into another book filled with information about the "Wild West." Day after day, she returned to the library, determined to absorb everything she possibly could, though she couldn't deny that the mission served in part as a distraction as she waited impatiently for a reply from Mr. King. Particularly now that she'd committed herself to such an enormous change, she was anxious for it to come to pass.

She had never known time to crawl by so slowly; the time that passed by since she'd sent the last letter feeling more like months rather than weeks. She resisted the urge to incorporate the post office into her daily errand schedule, knowing it would still be some time before a reply could be expected. And so, she continued to learn all that she could, branching out to learn about other foreign places when she'd read all she could about the west. The Caribbean sounded like a fascinating place, and she wondered if she would one day make a journey to England, thinking that visiting the place that her family came from would be exciting, too.

Finally, Olivia deemed that enough time had elapsed and made her way anxiously to the post office. The clerk there now knew her by name and was already searching for her mail by the time she arrived at the desk. Returning with a letter in tow, she thanked the clerk and darted out the door. She didn't wait this time, too impatient to hold back even the few moments it would take to reach her aunt's home. Instead, she stood in front of the post office with the envelope in her hand and opened it, recognizing the tidy writing on the page.

Dear Miss Collins,

I hope this letter finds you well. Your letter arrived in California at the most opportune time, providing me with a much-needed break from the laborious tasks that have occupied much of my time in recent weeks. My brothers and I have spent countless hours toiling in the soil, and while the land has rewarded us generously for our efforts, it is difficult, monotonous work that I am happy to escape from even briefly. Or perhaps it is my dear brother William whom I am relieved to escape temporarily.

Being unaccustomed to the work here, I believe he is not yet fully adjusted to the arduous labor. I do not mean it as an insult. He is, in fact, the most lighthearted of our small group, always ready with a witty retort or a humorous tale. I am quite certain that without him, our dinner table would be quite dull.

I am deeply sorry for the loss you suffered at such a young age. I had a sister for a brief amount of time whom I was very fond of, but I am sad to say she fell ill in her fifth year and did not live to see her sixth. It was a crushing blow, but my parents and brothers were there to console one another through that difficult time and while my family and I have not always seen eye to eye, I could not imagine not having them there to bicker with. I hope that your aunt has done what she could to ease your sorrow in some small way.

I confess that the winters in California were odd at first, being more accustomed to the cold and snow of New England all my life. It was particularly unsettling during my first Christmastime in San Francisco; there should have been snow on the ground and icicles adorning the rooftops, but instead it was hardly cool enough to light a fire. I am now far more accustomed to the warmer climate, but I do still miss the wintry scene outside my family's parlor each and every Christmas morning.

I must now be bold for a moment, Miss Collins. We have conversed for such a short time, but I feel confident already that this is a good match. If you feel the same, I would ask that you come to join me here in San Francisco. I have arranged for your passage, first to sail to the Panama Railway and then to San Francisco. This new route of travel means a much more comfortable voyage. It will take just a little more than a month to arrive rather than traveling by land which can equal a journey of as much as one hundred and forty days. It is my hope that we will have the opportunity to meet very soon.

Sincerely,

Jackson King

Suddenly the wait was over and the reality of the situation dawned on Olivia. She had been so anxious for this moment but now that it was upon her, she experienced a gripping moment of uncertainty. Was she really prepared to board a ship and leave Boston behind? Mr. King seemed well and fine in his letters, but what if he was truly a beast of a man, cajoling her into making the long trek to California.

"Breathe Olivia," she reminded herself, realizing that she'd been holding her breath since she began the final paragraph of Mr. King's letter.

As she stood there, breathing in and out slowly, her nerves calmed and she regained control over her wild thoughts. This was precisely the adventure she'd been hoping for all this time, and she wouldn't cower away from it now.

Unfortunately, if she was going to be leaving Boston, there was one more task she needed to tackle: Aunt Margaret. And since Olivia wasn't fond of procrastination, there wasn't any time better than the present. So, she headed home quickly, making it back in time for dinner with her aunt. She couldn't imagine her aunt's reaction; the woman had wanted her to marry since she was seventeen years old, but to a gold miner out west? Somehow Olivia doubted that was what Aunt Margaret had in mind all this time. Nevertheless, she'd given Olivia the freedom to turn down suitors and pursue her passion for learning. Would her aunt really deny her what she wanted so fervently now?

****

As she sat across the dining table from her aunt less than an hour later, Olivia took one more deep breath and opened her mouth. "Aunt Margaret? There is something I would like to discuss with you."

"Of course. What is it?" her aunt replied, lending Olivia her full attention.

"I wrote to a man in California some time ago, a response to an advertisement I read in the newspaper and in truth, I have been conversing with him ever since. We haven't written many letters, but I do believe he is a good match, Aunt Margaret." Olivia paused, allowing her aunt to process the information.

Her aunt just looked at her with a curious expression, apparently waiting for her niece to continue.

"The advertisement in the newspaper was for men out west looking for brides from the east. I believe that I have found a good match for marriage. In his last letter, the man has asked me to join him in San Francisco. He has made travel arrangements for me to embark on the next ship," Olivia finished, releasing the breath she again hadn't realized she'd been holding.

Her aunt was silent for another moment, the look on her face revealing absolutely nothing about what thoughts were running through her head. The awkward silence grew but Olivia waited patiently.

"Are you certain this is what you want? It seems to me an enormous decision, and an unexpected one from a girl who has rejected every suitor, the very notion of marriage since I've known her...wait...but it isn't the marriage that has you so enraptured, is it?" A knowing look settled on her aunt's face as a grin turned up the corners of her aging lips.

"And who may I ask is this man who has you venturing off across the country?" her aunt asked, still grinning.

"His name is Jackson King. He has been living in San Francisco, California for the past five years, but prior to that, his home was in Cambridge, Massachusetts. His parents still reside there, while his brothers have joined him out west," Olivia explained, easily recalling the details of Mr. King's letters.

"Did you say 'King'?" her aunt asked, intrigued.

"Um, yes. That is the name," she answered, though she wasn't certain if her aunt recognized the name or just hadn't been certain she'd heard her niece correctly.

"Oh dear. Son to Edward and Mary King from Cambridge, Massachusetts?" her aunt continued but Olivia couldn't remember Mr. King ever mentioning his father or mother's name.

"With four younger brothers, all of whom decided to follow their adventure-seeking eldest brother to the gold fields of California?" Aunt

Margaret met Olivia's gaze directly then, as if she were trying to read her niece's thoughts.

"How did you know that," Olivia queried.

"Why dear, I knew the Kings back when I was just a young girl. I nearly married Edward's older brother James, but his family found him a better match, I suppose, announcing his engagement to a young socialite from Jamestown," her aunt spoke sadly. "He's a widower now," her aunt said quietly, more to herself than to her niece.

Returning her attention to her niece, "Edward was a fine, young man, and we've met on occasion over the years. It was such a terribly tragedy the year he lost his only daughter. Mary had been so happy to finally have a little girl after producing so many fine, young boys for Edward." Her aunt was silent again, a sad, empathetic look on her face.

Olivia couldn't believe that the stranger she'd been writing letters to in California was the son of a man her aunt seemed to know so well. Nearly engaged to a member of the family? While the world took up a lot of space, it seemed so small sometimes. Did this improve or harm the chance that her aunt would approve of her choice? Was she bitter toward the King family? It didn't really sound like it.

"You have my blessing, Olivia," her aunt finally spoke. "Are you sure this is the right choice for you? It is a difficult life out in the west, and while I do believe the Kings have it easier than some of the rest, I cannot promise you that hardships will never come."

"I am sure this is what I want. You know I could never be content in a marriage here, and the same life day in and day out could do nothing but bore me to tears. Mr. King is offering something so much more than marriage; adventure, excitement, new experiences...the unknown," Olivia finished, exhilaration evident in her eyes.

"I am going to miss you terribly, but it appears that you two are most certainly well-suited for one another," Aunt Margaret rolled her eyes good-naturedly.

"I'm going to miss you, too." Olivia rose from her seat, moving to wrap her arms around her aunt, part in gratitude and part in sorrow.

As much as she wanted this adventure, she was genuinely sad to be leaving the only family she had known for so many years, but now that she had her aunt's approval, the only thing left to do was pack. The next ship left in just under one week, so there was very little time to prepare. Finishing dinner, she let aunt Margaret's maid take care of the cleaning that evening, heading off to her room and pulling a suitcase from her closet—the very same suitcase that she had brought with her from her parents' home when she came to live with her aunt.

Opening it up, she ran her fingers across the contents carefully. While a great deal of the belongings from her old home were packed and directed under the care of aunt Margaret, Olivia had crept throughout the house before her aunt had arrived, stashing her mother's favorite bonnet and heirloom locket in her suitcase, along with her father's favorite books, her brother's toy soldiers and the puppets her mother had made for Olivia and her brother. She had never once taken the precious items out of the suitcase, but she had pulled out the luggage and looked at them often, particularly during the first several months after coming to live with her aunt. She wouldn't disturb them now either, carefully folding and packing her belongings from her room on top of her family keepsakes.

Just thirty minutes later, Olivia was finished. All of the things she wanted to bring with her had been packed and there were no more preparations that needed to be made. It seemed odd that she could so easily pack up her entire life and be ready to move across the country in thirty minutes, but it was true nevertheless, and now all she had to do was figure out how to make it through an entire week of waiting.

She had just settled on a book to help her pass through the evening hours when a knock sounded quietly at her door.

"Come in," she called, laying the book face down on the table in front of her to keep her page as her aunt walked into the room.

She looked terribly uncomfortable, and so Olivia waited patiently, her aunt coming to sit down beside her without saying a word. They sat there silently for a moment, then two, when finally Aunt Margaret cleared her throat, turning to face Olivia as she began to speak.

"When your parents passed away, Olivia, you were far too young to worry about money and finances, of course. Then, as the years went by, it seemed an unnecessary discussion for us to have. Certainly, your lack of interest in marriage made me feel comfortable in keeping it to myself for the time being," her aunt began cryptically.

"Now that circumstances have changed, I think it is time to have this conversation. You see, your parents did not leave you penniless, Olivia. I had intended to set the money aside as a dowry for you, but given that you've gone ahead and made your own match, I think it should be yours to use as you see fit. But, I caution you, that once you are married, you must understand that anything that once belonged to you, would then belong to your husband. Hide it, bury it, or be absolutely certain that the man you are going to marry will not abuse or squander what you have."

Aunt Margaret's piercing gaze told Olivia she was trying to read her thoughts yet again, but in truth, Olivia didn't know what to think. She had known that her parents had been relatively well off, but never thought much about it once she moved to her aunt's home. Certainly it couldn't be much, or her aunt would have been able to live in the lap of luxury all this time, rather than in moderate comfort.

"Olivia, do you understand?" her aunt broke into her silent thoughts, her hand coming to rest firmly on top of her niece's.

Olivia nodded uncertainly. Handing her niece a satchel, Aunt Margaret spoke in a hushed tone, as if she worried a passerby on the street might be listening to her conversation.

"You are the sole heiress of a sum of thirty thousand pounds, Olivia, and that is before the property that has remained in the family's name."

Olivia did her best to prevent her jaw from dropping to the floor. It was a veritable fortune. She could live independently and never want for anything; travel the world in comfort...but she realized in that moment that she didn't want to travel alone, venture to the far ends of the earth by herself. Though she had never given it much consideration prior to responding to Mr. King's advertisement, the idea of marriage had grown upon her throughout the past several months. The prospect of a life partner to share her adventures with sounded far more appealing than a life of solitude. While the fortune certainly did come as a shock, it didn't matter if she had all the money in the world, she didn't want to venture through it alone. And whether due to her own stubbornness in sticking to her decision or some higher power at work, marriage to Mr. King still felt like the right choice for her. He felt like the right choice.

****

The week passed quickly and before she knew it, Olivia was wrapping her arms around her aunt, bidding farewell to the woman who had taken care of her as her own for so many years. And though she still felt sadness to her core at leaving her aunt behind, her determination never faltered. She stepped onto the ship a few moments later, waving goodbye once more from up above and allowed the man who greeted her there to lead her to her quarters, although she didn't spend much time there, too fascinated with the roiling waters beneath the ship once it headed away from the docks. In fact, Olivia spent nearly the entire voyage looking out at the vast ocean, captivated by the gentle waves, the sun rising and setting on the horizon, the sea life that would reach the water's surface every now and then, and the vast number of birds that would flock by overhead whenever the ship was near land. Later, crossing the canal, she was told what a comfortable and quick alternative it was to the once grueling trek through the forest. She was happy it was quicker, but she wondered if the adventure of the forest would have been more exciting than the comfort of the sailing vessel.

Before she knew it, she was boarding the ship for the last leg of her trip, which would take her straight to San Francisco and Mr. Jackson King. Though shorter than the trip from New England to Panama, this last voyage seemed to drag on forever as her anxiousness to reach the end of her journey increased. She spotted the docks long before the ship glided into port. Once there, she grabbed hold of her belongings, making her way across the deck while watching the crowd assemble below.

Descending the stairs to the docks below, Olivia looked around, realizing that she had no practical way of identifying Mr. King in the crowd. Then she saw him—she was certain it was him, though she had no idea how. He stood out from the rest of the men huddled around the docks, a half a foot taller than the rest. He was looking up at the boat, his vivid emerald eyes searching for something. As his eyes found her, his expression changed and she swore she saw his gaze begin to burn with emerald fire. As swiftly as the flames ignited, they were extinguished, the man's search continuing along the length of the boat. Olivia stood there watching him, mesmerized. He was by far the most attractive man she'd ever laid eyes upon. Perhaps it was only wishful thinking that had her certain he was Mr. King. Every young maiden dreams of a handsome knight, but that doesn't make such silly dream a reality.

His gaze continued its search, making its way back to her. As his eyes settled on her this time, recognition dawned there, and she knew it wasn't wishful thinking. She started toward him, descending the few remaining steps as Mr. King made his way toward her slowly through the crowd. The disconcerted expression he wore concerned her; she would have guessed that he was unhappy with her in some way, but the heated look in his eyes from just a moment before suggested otherwise. Confusing, for sure.

"Miss Collins?" the man asked, coming to stand about two feet in front of her.

"I am. And you must be Mr. King," she replied, forcing a kind smile on her face, though a multitude of emotions roiled within her. She had tried to prepare herself for this moment, but her preparations had assumed an ordinary man, not this incredibly handsome stranger who had looked at her with a fiery gaze that did odd things to her composure.

"I am pleased to meet you. I trust that your journey was comfortable," he continued cordially.

"It is a pleasure to make your acquaintance...finally," Olivia added in afterthought, thinking of all the things she knew about this man already, even though they had only met in person this very moment. He smiled then, and if she thought he couldn't possibly be any more attractive, she'd been wrong.

"It is an odd thing, is it not? To meet after becoming acquainted already?" Mr. King confessed aloud one of her own thoughts, and Olivia nodded in agreement.

A moment later, she spotted another man making his way through the crowd toward them. The familial resemblance was undeniable, but this man was younger and while Mr. King appeared to be broad and muscular, this man was far more lanky.

"I'm sorry, Jackson. But I could not remain with the horses any longer. I had to catch a glimpse of the woman who has finally felled my bachelor brother. And you must be she," the man announced, turning to face Olivia. His appreciative gaze told her he approved of at least some of her "aspects," though he was quick to cover his response.

"Miss Collins, it is an honor to meet you. Let me introduce myself. My name is William King and I am the youngest of the King Brothers. I would like to tell you that you have made a good choice in my brother, but dear Miss Collins, can you not see that there is something wrong with us Kings? All five of us crazy enough to leave the comfort of New England for the excitement of the Wild West. I may in fact be a much more reasonable choice, as I at least had the good sense to hold out the longest," William finished his flamboyant speech.

Olivia could tell immediately that he was a young, charismatic man who would no doubt become a good friend. She liked him already.

"It is a pleasure to meet you, Mr. King. While I appreciate your candor, I believe my mind is made up," she smiled graciously.

"Alright William. Why don't you make yourself useful and lead the way back to the carriage," Jackson cut in, likely reining in William's colorful greeting before he made a fool of himself.

William nodded, turning back into the crowd and stretching out his arms wide to clear a path. Olivia covered her mouth to hide a giggle in response to the silly scene before her, but given the clear walkway his action provided, she certainly wouldn't complain. She even saw Jackson's brief smile from the corner of her eye before he offered his arm to guide Olivia through the now open walkway. It only took a moment to reach the carriage, set back just thirty steps from the docks.

The two men waited as she climbed into the carriage, William stealing the seat next to her before Jackson could object. Though, it seemed he was more than content to be maintaining his distance, an odd look still occupying his features, as if he felt something wasn't quite right here, or perhaps not what he had expected. William monopolized the majority of the conversation throughout the ride, talking mostly about the differences between the east and west since his move there. He spoke a little about the other King Brothers; the second youngest, James, who idolized Jackson, the pragmatic second eldest, Joseph, and Thomas, the middle brother who spent a bit too much time occupied with pleasing others—a result of his kind-hearted nature.

But it was Jackson King's personality that definitely intrigued her the most. He was the adventurous of the brothers, but there was every bit as much a down to earth side to him as well. He was committed to anything he set himself to, working tirelessly to see it come to fruition. The dedicated adventurer? Olivia would have thought it an impossible combination if it hadn't been a near identical rendition of her own personality.

Jackson cleared his throat before his brother could launch further into breaking down every aspect of his character, turning to point out the carriage window at the row of houses up ahead. "You've chattered on the entire way home, William. How about a moment of peace and quiet for Miss Collins before we arrive?" he asked, though it in no way sounded like a question.

Olivia turned to follow Jackson's gaze out the window and was surprised by what she found there. Indeed a row of houses stood not a hundred feet away, but they were not what she had expected. She had read about the rustic cottages serving as homes to many miners out west and had anticipated adjusting to monumental changes in her accommodations. And while the houses weren't quite as magnificent as the grand estates back in the east, they were positively lovely homes. The last in the row of four was much larger than the rest, covering at least as much as two of the other houses put together. The beginnings of another house were laid out beyond the large house as if construction had just begun on this last one but it was still some way before completion. The carriage passed by the first three houses, coming to a halt in front of the larger one-on-one

"Now, you'll be on your best behavior William. Or I'll send you to sleep in your own house tonight." Jackson spoke sternly to his brother, but the light dancing in his eyes told her he was teasing. "So, he does have a sense of humor after all," Olivia thought to herself, pleased by the small revelation.

The two brothers descended the steps from the carriage and Jackson offered his hand to Olivia in assistance. Once firmly on the ground, she let her gaze roam across the houses in front of her. In the large house, there were a multitude of windows that let light in from every side and a veranda that wrapped around three sides of the house.

"I suppose if I was going to live beneath the California sun, I was going to make the most of it," Jackson offered in explanation.

"It's beautiful, Mr. King. I hadn't expected..." she let the thought trail off, figuring there was no kind way of finishing it. Jackson nodded, but she could tell the unperturbed visage he wore was fake, and she worried that she had offended him. Before she could attempt to correct the situation, her eyes were drawn elsewhere, noticing that the porches on the other houses were no longer empty. A man and a woman stood on the porch of each house, each peering in her direction.

"My brothers and their wives," Jackson explained before Olivia could pose the question. She was quiet then, but her face was suddenly alight, watching as a handful of children filed out of the houses and onto the porches. Most of them barely tall enough to see over the railings, the eldest of them could not have been more than four years old. Apparently at that age, curiosity won out it seemed over the need for decorum or the possibility of reprimand, as the youngster came racing toward the carriage at a pace Olivia was quite certain no adult could match. The child managed to bring herself to a halt just steps away from barreling head first into the group.

"Is this her, uncle Jackson?" the young girl asked excitedly. "It is, isn't it," she continued without a pause.

"This is Miss Collins," Jackson affirmed, picking up the child like she weighed no more than a feather. "May I introduce you to the young Miss Caroline King," he continued, addressing Olivia.

"It is a pleasure to meet you, Miss King," Olivia greeted happily.

"Are you going to stop Uncle Jackson from sowing wild oats?" Caroline asked innocently. "I don't know why mother dislikes oats so much," the child thought aloud, forcing William to smother a chuckle.

"Perhaps your mother speaks too much of oats," Jackson admonished lightly, and then turned his attention to the oncoming crowd of men, women and children.

Olivia didn't have long to contemplate Mr. King's wild oats before her attention was directed toward the myriad of introductions that began. All of

Jackson King's brothers and their wives seemed perfectly cordial, and the children were delightful. The two women married to the older King Brothers, Clara and Annie, were both daughters of miners in the area. Each of them at least seven or eight years older than Olivia. The woman, Elizabeth, married to the second youngest brother was also from Boston and not more than three or four years older. She was prettier than the other two, but still of a rather sturdy frame. Olivia felt an immediate fondness for Elizabeth who chose to venture out west with her family several years ago, rather than settling for a loveless marriage proposal back home.

"Jackson, I'm going to take Miss Collins to her room so she can get settled in. You feel free to send this horde back to work," Elizabeth smiled, grabbing hold of Olivia's hand and tugging her through the crowd and up the steps of the large house.

"Should I be staying here?" Olivia asked in a slight panic once out of earshot. "I mean, if this is Mr. King's house, then wouldn't it be somewhat improper for me to reside here?"

"Oh, don't worry about propriety here. We certainly aren't wondering about Jackson's virtue, and between William and the rest of us, we'll be around to ensure yours stays intact," Elizabeth assured her.

Olivia's curiosity would have compelled her to inquire further about Mr. King, but her attention was drawn elsewhere once again as Elizabeth opened the front door, revealing the simple yet elegant décor within. The home wasn't cluttered with elaborate tapestries and trinkets, but the clean lines throughout made the home appear even larger inside. Elizabeth ascended the tall staircase and Olivia followed behind, leading her to the left once they reached the top to a room two doors from the stairs. There were two more doors on the opposite side of the staircase, Jackson's and William's she presumed. Elizabeth stood back, motioning for Olivia to enter her new room and she was immediately amazed by the difference she found within.

"I took the liberty of dressing up your room a little. Jackson's decorating style leans toward the simplistic, as I'm sure you've noticed," Elizabeth explained. The room was beautiful, with an ornate tapestry adorning the wall, a cozy rug at the foot of the bed, a pile of books stacked on the table next to the bed and candlesticks and trinkets adorning the tabletops and window sills.

"Do you like it here?" Olivia piped up before Elizabeth could leave the room.

"At first it was an adjustment, I must admit. Clara and Annie weren't sure what to think of me early on, and I felt the need to work to fit in. But I've grown very fond of San Francisco, and they really are fine women and besides, it is different for you. You've come here to marry Jackson, the leader of the pact, so to speak. No one would dare give you a hard time.

Now that you are here, I am quite certain we will be great friends. You'll have an ally right from the start," she smiled conspiratorially.

"I believe you are right, but I am not so certain that Mr. King feels the same way. He seems rather cold...not rude, I assure you, but distant and uninterested. I don't see how I could have offended him," Olivia expressed her confusion.

"Oh, never mind him. I do believe he was expecting someone a little...different, nut he will come around. Just look at you; how could he not?" Elizabeth tried to reassure her.

"Different? I don't understand."

"I shouldn't have said anything. I'm sure it will all work out just fine. He is a good man, Olivia. Almost as good as he is handsome," Elizabeth smiled devilishly.

Olivia couldn't help but smile, too, remembering her response to him not long ago on the docks.

"Alright then. One of the men will bring up your luggage shortly. You go ahead and get freshened up. Dinner will be ready shortly, so please join us downstairs when you're ready," Elizabeth explained, smiling kindly once more before leaving.

Olivia listened to her footsteps as she descended the staircase, but before she had a full moment to herself, footsteps sounded on the stairs once again. The heavier steps told her it was likely one of the men bringing her luggage so she moved to meet them at the door, but quickly found herself tongue-tied as Jackson King appeared in the doorway, her luggage in tow and a book in his free hand.

"I have something for you, Miss Collins," he stated simply, holding out the book to her.

Surprised, she took it, running her fingers over the cover before opening it up. Inside, she found page upon page of maps, all marked by the paths and trails taken by different explorers. She came upon a page of America, from east to west, and on it were two hand drawn outlines.

"This is the route I took from my home in Cambridge," he explained pointing to one of the lines. "The other is the route you took from Boston. Our first adventures to San Francisco. From your letters, I thought you might like it," he finished.

"It's wonderful, Mr. King. Thank you," Olivia beamed brightly. It really was the most perfect gift, more thoughtful than she could have ever imagined.

"Please, if we are going to be married, I believe you can call me Jackson," he told her, though that disconcerted look flitted across his features briefly as he spoke.

"Then you should most certainly call me Olivia," she offered back, trying to ignore the inkling of concern resounding in her head.

She didn't know why, but her future husband was not happy with this match. Perhaps it was all well and good in letter, but now that she was there, he seemed to be reconsidering giving up his bachelorhood. What would she do then? Go back to Boston? Certainly, no. She'd left that life behind her, but she had intended to leave it for a new life with Mr. King. A woman on her own in the west? That sounded questionable at best.

"Will you join us for dinner then, Olivia?" he asked in a quieter tone.

The change caught her attention, and she looked up, meeting his gaze. There were so many conflicting emotions there, it was almost dizzying. Discontent warred with desire, and she couldn't imagine for the life of her why he was displeased, but how was one to broach the subject? It seemed poor manners after meeting the man just a few hours before.

"I will," she replied, forcing her lips to curve upward in a gentle smile.

She expected him to leave then, but instead he lingered, standing silently in the doorway to her new room. He looked at her, as if he was contemplating something, but just as it looked as if he might speak, he turned, descending the stairs quickly. He was certainly becoming the most confusing man she'd ever met, she thought to herself before returning her attention to the book of maps, tracing the outline the two of them traveled to their current location. She smiled before placing the book carefully on the bed, freshening up quickly and then heading downstairs.

The group was only just then heading toward the large dining room, Elizabeth grabbing hold of her hand and pulling her along to sit side by side, next to the head of the table. Jackson sat at the head and William sat across from Olivia, entertaining the group throughout dinner with childhood stories, adolescent dreams and a few improper antics about their early beginnings as men. Jackson didn't appear the least bit pleased as William not-so-subtle insinuated about a number of dalliances with less than proper women and he cut him off entirely before his young brother could begin to recount each tale. The conversation turned to mining and life in San Francisco, and Olivia was absolutely amazed by the amount of effort Jackson had put into the venture already, working nearly seven days a week to establish a profit as quickly as possible, and spending carefully, unlike so many other bachelor miners seemed prone to do in the area.

She retired to bed not long after dinner, feeling fatigued early from her lengthy travels, but as the sun arose in the sky early the next morning, she awoke with a renewed vigor, delving into every aspect of her new life that she could. She attempted to learn the process of mining gold, helped out around the houses with cooking and cleaning, and found herself enthralled with the children, reading the younger ones stories and playing games with Caroline and her three-year-old brother. Around noon time, not seeing any of the men return for a meal, she enlisted Elizabeth's help in fixing a picnic lunch like those her mother would prepare for her and her brother long ago. The two of them walked the short distance to where the men were mining, and while most of the group was boisterously pleased by the brief break, Jackson's expression still told Olivia he was not entirely content. Though, he seemed happy enough to dig into the food she had brought, making her feel like her efforts were not entirely wasted.

The two of them dined alone together that evening, and while the conversation started off stilted, the ease in which they conversed in letters overtook them before long. Jackson shared his version of his childhood story; the young boy never settled with the notion of a life behind his desk—his father owned a small shipping company, expecting Jackson to follow in his footsteps. And while the prospect of spending a life at sea sounded full of adventure, his father spent most of his time hampered with paper work and making shipping arrangements. He was certain even then that there was something more out there for him, and from the moment he'd heard about men venturing off to make a life for themselves out west, he knew it was what he wanted.

It was Olivia's turn then, recounting her happy, yet uneventful childhood; the most adventurous tale was her trip to her aunt's home in Boston every year. It was difficult for her to speak about her parents and her brother, but somehow it was easier to talk to Jackson about her sad memories than anyone she'd ever known. He reached out a hand, resting it on top of hers in condolence as she spoke. A kind gesture, but the moment his fingers came in contact with her soft skin, she felt tiny tremors of something she'd never experienced before course up her arm. It was distracting to say the least, but she forced her mind to remain on the conversation as best as she could.

****

Her first few days in San Francisco sped by in a flash and suddenly she had been there for weeks, finding her groove in daily life and confirming that she'd been right in her decision; she was far happier in this foreign, barren land than she'd ever been in the teeming city of Boston. Her conversations with Jackson were stimulating and exciting, just as she had imagined, but there was still something not quite right. That same, discontent look she'd seen in Jackson's eyes remained there almost constantly, telling her he was not nearly as happy with this arrangement.

Nevertheless, the wedding date was set; on December twenty-fifth, of the year 1856, she would become his wife, Mrs. Olivia King. The first of December had already come and gone, and though it didn't feel like Christmastime was nearing—the unseasonably warm weather in comparison to New England—a Christmas wedding seemed like the most perfect way to celebrate the holiday.

Elizabeth began to fuss over decorations and a wedding dress, and Olivia was happy to go along with the preparations, so long as the fussing stopped at precisely noon each day. It had become her daily routine to take lunch out to the brothers, preparing a separate basket full of food for her and Jackson so that the two of them could separate from the group, continuing whatever conversation they had begun the afternoon or evening prior. He was no longer just the means to an adventure for her. Through watching him and through their conversations, she'd begun to see that he was a strong and dedicated man, hard-working, considerate, and he loved his family with a quiet passion that was evident in everything he did. She had only been hoping for a companion who could carry on a reasonable conversation when she'd decided to move out west, but now, she loved so many different aspects about him that she wouldn't care if he was mute—she'd be happy to sit there in silence with him.

Of course, she couldn't tell Jackson such things; the discontentedness that radiated from his gaze served to keep her at bay, hiding her emotions beneath the surface. She couldn't help but wonder if he would rather she had never come...perhaps he would up and one day send her away.

As their wedding day approached, it seemed less likely, their conversations continuing in the usual way, no sign of a concrete end in sight. As the morning of their wedding arrived, Olivia breathed a sigh of relief, rising out of bed. He hadn't sent her on her way. In fact, he'd sent the house to bed early last evening in preparation for today's grand event. She freshened up quickly, seeing that the sun was already high in the sky, and just as she was about to descend the stairs for breakfast, Elizabeth came bursting into the room.

"Oh no. You're not going anywhere. We'll have you ready in no time.

The bride and groom are not supposed to see each other before the wedding, my family tradition says," she explained, and the tone of her voice told Olivia there was no point in arguing.

Sitting back down, she sat patiently as Elizabeth brushed and twined her hair, pinched her cheeks and helped her slip into the beautiful white dress she'd made by hand for this occasion. Nearly a full hour later, and she announced that Olivia was indeed ready.

"Now may I get my breakfast?" Olivia queried teasingly, knowing Elizabeth meant well.

"The ceremony is supposed to be in an hour, but everyone is already here...nobody seems to know what to do with a day off around here. My James was up at the crack of dawn, determined to get some work in early. Can you believe it?" she exclaimed.

Olivia was already on her feet, determined to make her way to the kitchen before making her way down the aisle. "I'm sure everyone will manage for another few minutes," she told her, slipping out the door and down the stairs, turning her head to see if Elizabeth was following behind her. As she turned back to watch her step down the final stair, she came face to face with Jackson, standing alone in the front foyer. She went to open her mouth, chastising him for seeing the bride before the wedding in good jest, but the look on his face forced her words to catch in her throat. The discontentedness was not confined to his eyes but rather he wore it all over his face. For some reason, all of the talk of his virtue and the dalliances with improper ladies sprung to mind, and amid a wave of jealousy, Olivia also couldn't help but to wonder if perhaps the notion of marriage was not sitting well with him.

"You are not happy." She finally worked up the nerve to state it plainly, gently demanding that the issue come to light.

He was silent. "If you are not content, Jackson, let us discuss it now. Look at how well we've been getting on. Do you think I would want you to be unhappy?"

He was silent for another moment, but then, "You should not have come here," Jackson's husky voice sounded pained. "Look at you, Olivia. You're barely older than a child. And look at your hands...they were certainly not made for the hard work that is perpetually required here. You are the epitome of femininity; you should be on the arm of a socialite in a parlor in Boston, not working in the soil or as a servant in San Francisco."

Olivia didn't know how to respond. Was this the way he would end their engagement? On the day of their wedding, trying to convince her it was she who did not want to be there.

"Intelligent, adventurous...that is what my ad said. These were not things that should have caught the attention of a young lady; I expected you to be...older...plainer...a companion to work alongside, not one who would distract me to wit's end. You've seen my brothers' wives. Elizabeth is the most comely of them all, and she pales in comparison to you, Olivia. You are beautiful, intelligent, kind...all things that should not be wasted here."

"But, I want to be here...with you," she replied softly. "Remember my letters? I wanted adventure all along Jackson, and I was not foolish enough to think it would come easily. At first, it was only the adventure that occupied my thoughts, swayed my decision. But then I read your letters and I traveled to San Francisco. And now I fear it is not only the adventure that I want," she paused, taking a deep breath and forcing herself to continue. "I want you, as a partner, as a companion, a fellow adventurer, and in ways I cannot confess." Olivia blushed lightly, remembering all of the times she'd gazed at his broad muscular chest, his full lips, his strong hands...

Shaking her head to clear it, she thought of the satchel stilled tucked away neatly in her suitcase, and it gave her an idea. Reaching out, she grabbed hold of his hands.

"Please stay right here," she beseeched him, and then turned, darting up the stairs to her room above and returning with the satchel a moment later.

She took a deep breath, collecting her thoughts and then held out the bag. "I am not here because I have to be, Jackson." It felt odd to use his name so easily, but she liked the way it felt on her tongue.

"I could have stayed in New England if that was my wish. Even when I arrived here, I could have changed my mind and headed home, or gone out on my own, but I have liked it here so much...I have liked being here with you so much, that I completely forgot that this even existed."

She motioned for him to take the satchel, but when he didn't reach for it immediately, she placed it in his hands, opening the strings that held it closed herself and pulling up handfuls of the money contained within.

"You see? There is nothing holding me here but you. I could have kept this hidden from you, saved it to make my escape if I was unhappy. But I am happy. There is thirty thousand pounds in this satchel. It is for you... for us... for your brothers... for Elizabeth... Caroline. You have made a life here; turned this barren land into something wonderful. I want to be a part of this adventure with you," Olivia finished emphatically.

Jackson was speechless for a moment, and she desperately wished she could read his thoughts, decipher the emotions in his eyes. She wondered if he was angry, upset that she had hidden such a large sum from him.

"You could have lived a life of luxury, but instead you would rather live here with me?"

He spoke so quietly it was difficult to read the emotion in his tone, and his question sounded more like a statement to Olivia. She nodded anyway. She didn't know what to think, but in the next moment as his lips pressed hard against hers, all thoughts fled her mind. The satchel dropped to the floor as his hands wrapped around her waist, and suddenly her world felt right.

"Ahem," a voice interrupted from behind. Jackson was first to pull away as every part of Olivia was absorbed in the feel of his lips against hers. She blushed once his lips left hers, realizing a crowd had assembled in the hallway behind them.

"I believe you are supposed to save that part for after the ceremony," Elizabeth spoke, smiling devilishly from a few stairs above them. "But these King men are hard to resist, aren't they?"

Jackson looked down at Olivia then, a question in his eyes. She nodded, and he smiled before turning to address the crowd. "Then should we not get this wedding underway lest my eager bride compromise my virtue just moments before the vows are spoken?" he teased.

As the group made their way into the parlor, Jackson stopped, staring out the window. "You did it...you actually did it! It's snowing on Christmas just as you had longed for!" he exclaimed quietly. Puzzled, Olivia turned to follow his gaze. Snow; softly falling from the sky, slowly blanketing the barren front yard. "You brought snow with you from New England, as you said you would," he smiled, leaning down to kiss her lips gently.

"Ahem," Elizabeth sounded from just behind them.

"Right. Virtue. I suggest we hurry then," Olivia teased, her lips brushing against Jackson's as she spoke.

ELIZABETH'S CHRISTMAS MIRACLE

Boston, Massachusetts - 1866

Life kept getting harder and harder for Elizabeth Beaumont and her family. The belief had been that, with the war over, things would be peaceful and go back to the way they were before, but her Dear husband Richard was gone now, along with so many other husbands, fathers and sons. She tried her best not to dwell on thoughts of the toll that the war had had on everyone, but it was impossible to avoid. Her two young children, Anne and Willie, were left without a father and Elizabeth was left alone with too many bills and debts to be paid.

During the war, Elizabeth worked as a nurse in a Boston military hospital, helping to heal the wounded veterans who were returning from the war mostly not in one piece. It had not been pleasant, nor had it been the sort of thing she wanted to do with her life, but she was glad all the same that she had been able to be there and help, and earn steady pay, instead of sitting at home fretting. Once the war ended and the surviving men returned to their jobs, her work was no longer needed at the hospital. That broke her heart more than she expected. With men around to fill all of the available positions, Elizabeth had no means to make a living for herself and take care of her family and her home.

She tried selling valuables, but she could not afford to part with more than a few things. Once that option dried up, she could only think of two choices left to her, one of which made her blush just thinking of it. She could not become one of *those* women. She would not subject herself or her children to that. One option remained. She had heard other widows speaking of it in hushed voices at the hospital. She could remarry a stranger out west.

It was a surprising notion to think of, but it also made a lot of sense to her. There were many men who were working out west who had everything they could ever need: gold, land, independence. The only thing they did not have was the love and companionship of a woman. Despite any apprehension she felt about it, Elizabeth picked up the newspaper and went in search of the advertisements.

The first to catch her attention was posted by a widower in California named Frederick O'Connell. The tale that he told reminded her of her own sad story. He had lost his wife Charlotte to Tuberculosis the previous year, and he had two young boys that he was left to care for by himself. He was hoping to find *a kind woman to be a mother to my children and a friend to me.*

Elizabeth immediately empathized with his desire for companionship. To have found someone to love and be loved by, and then lose them was one of the most personal tragedies one could experience. No one should go through that alone.

She quickly took up a pen and some paper to write a letter in response to Frederick O'Connell. She blushed a bit, ruminating on the fact that she was now, in essence, applying to be some far off gentleman's bride. She wondered if it would make the courtship easier, as it would be relieving her of the day-to-day nervousness that went with meeting suitors. Richard often made delightful remarks about her beauty, but this gentleman would be judging her, at first, almost exclusively on her choice of words.

She bit her lip, smiling down at the so-far blank parchment on her desk.

"What are you doing, Mama?" her daughter Anne asked, coming into the room dressed in her white nightgown and carrying her teddy bear by its ear. She was eight years old, and she and her five-year-old brother Willie were supposed to be asleep. As usual, at least Willie was following instructions.

Elizabeth set down her pen and gave Anne a small smile. "I'm writing a letter to a friend. What do you think you are doing? You are supposed to be in bed for the night, young lady."

Anne awkwardly crawled up into her mother's lap. "Is your friend going to come see us?" she asked.

Elizabeth gave Anne's gold curls a pat. "Perhaps," she said. "Would you like that?"

The little girl nodded.

"Good," Elizabeth replied. "In the meantime, your mama would like you to go to sleep." Carefully, she stood up, holding the child in her arms. She carried Anne back to the children's bed chamber and gently tucked her back into bed.

Willie was fast asleep. Elizabeth hoped that the children's dreams were untroubled. She knew that Willie in particular had taken their father's death very hard. He had only been three years old when Richard died, but little boys needed their fathers. Anne had been Richard's bright star to coo over, and it was clear that the girl missed having such a doting figure in her life. Elizabeth did her best, but she could not be two parents at once.

She sat on the edge of Anne's bed and petted her daughter's head until, at last, Anne was asleep.

Quietly, Elizabeth walked back out to her desk in the sitting room and sat down to her letter.

Dear Mr. O'Connell,

It grieved me to read of your wife's passing and the loneliness and melancholy you have suffered. My name is Elizabeth Beaumont and I too have felt the sharp pain of bereavement these past two years. My late husband, Mr. Richard Beaumont, was in the 57th Massachusetts Infantry and fell during the battle at Spotsylvania. Words cannot adequately express the gaping emptiness that this loss has left in my life, or the lives of my children.

I know that words alone cannot help to staunch the wounds of this sadness. I offer to you my understanding, my support and my friendship in this your time of need.

May this letter of mine find you well and I shall anticipate your response. In the meantime, I shall pray for you and your children.

With warmest regards,

Mrs. Elizabeth Beaumont

Going through one of her photograph albums, Elizabeth selected a portrait of herself to send to her new suitor. In the photograph, she was dressed in a pretty white dress with a light flower pattern atop the bodice. Her long, brown curls were loose and hung down well past her shoulders. She appeared to be young and in love. Elizabeth hoped that it would not give Frederick O'Connell the wrong impression of her age. The portrait was taken in 1860, before the war and during the marriage to her husband, when she was twenty-two. As she recalled languidly, the photograph was taken at Richard's request. He was still a part of the big moments in her life even now…

Carefully, Elizabeth placed the portrait into the envelope intended for Frederick O'Connell. She sealed the letter in as well and addressed the envelope to Mr. O'Connell's home in Douglas City, California. Now that she had written the letter to him, she began to feel excited at the prospect of a new friend. She hoped that he would be interested in starting a correspondence with her. It had been over ten years since she last had a beau for which to pose for portraits and to fill her mind with giddy fantasies. She prayed that the letter would reach him swiftly and he would write back to her.

****

Time, of course, did not stand still while Elizabeth waited for a letter to arrive from California. The children went to and from school and the landlord of their building dropped in, every afternoon like clockwork, to remind her that she still needed to deliver her rent payments.

"I remember, Mr. Thompson," she said in a pleading tone. "I am working very hard to get it to you. Times have been difficult ever since my husband's passing."

Mr. Thompson took off his cap, as he always did when the late Mr. Beaumont was mentioned. Elizabeth sometimes believed that Mr. Thompson had more respect for the dead man than he did for the living widow.

"I understand, Mrs. Beaumont," the landlord said solemnly. Post the payment to me, and I will trouble you no further. I am aware that times are hard. Times are hard for all of us these days. Might you perhaps take out a loan in the meantime?"

Elizabeth sighed and shook her head. "I suppose I could," she said sadly. She was quickly running out of options. She could not afford to move out of her apartment, and she could not expect the man she had not even met yet to step in and whisk her and her children away to California with him. It would be too much to hope let alone ask for.

She checked her mailbox as soon as the landlord left her, and discovered to her sheer delight that there was a letter inside from California! Rushing back into her apartment, she carefully opened the envelope with a pair of scissors as not to disturb its contents.

Inside, there was a photograph of a young man with dashing good looks. He had blond hair and a handsome, well-chiseled face with a neat beard and mustache. He was dressed in an outfit that made it appear as though he was about to go riding. Elizabeth imagined him riding off to fight the fearful dragon of debt and save her from her lonely tower. She smiled down at the photograph in her hands for several moments before realizing that she must read the letter and see what wondrous words awaited her there.

My Dear Mrs. Beaumont,

How unfortunate that one as lovely as you should be left alone in the world! But how proud of your late husband you must be as well. It seems to me that he was quite valiant to have fought in the war. Meanwhile, I packed up my bags and headed west. You must not think me too selfish. I knew that my worth was not on the battlefield, but in whatever business lay ahead. The little action I did see left me wounded, though more in mind than in body. So I admire the late Mr. Beaumont. I feel privileged and a small amount of shame that you have enquired after my advertisement, knowing that you have loved someone so highly esteemed.

Let us not speak any more of that for now. Please let me read more about you. What do you like to do to while away the hours? Have you ever been atop a horse? I own a ranch here with horses, and I am quite fond of riding. I also own a gold mining company, but I do not let any dust and dirt into my home so you can rest assured that you will find only cleanliness around my property. My late wife was always a perfectionist when it came to that.

When I originally landed here in Douglas City, times were hard and money was tight. I am not afraid to boast that I have prospered out here. I do believe that I'd make a fine husband and a good father, too. If you could find it in your heart, please write to me again. I will await your letter most eagerly.

With fondness,

Frederick O'Connell

Elizabeth read over the letter three times. Each time made her giddier than the last. Mr. O'Connell sounded so charming and his lifestyle was so different from what she was accustomed to. She was enchanted by the idea of going out west and living like a rancher's wife. If they did indeed proceed with this, she would be a rancher's wife! All of her current troubles would go away. Surely she would have troubles in California as well. Troubles were everywhere. Oh, but it would be an adventure! After everything that had happened in her life, she was ready to explore and find something new.

She was struck by his guilt about not being a soldier like her late husband. If anything, she felt relief to have found a gentleman who was not a part of that cruel and life-altering affair. Richard had not truly been a soldier at heart. He had been a young lawyer called to the war because of his country, not because of any desire to fight. Elizabeth knew that, if he had had the choice, he would never have fought at all. She did not want Frederick to think for one moment that he had anything to feel guilty about.

The children rushed home soon after from school. Willie leap up and hugged his mother as she scooped him up and gave him a kiss. She wished that she could tell him and Anne about Mr. O'Connell, but she was not sure it was the right time. They would be confused, and she did not want to let them know of any changes prematurely. There was a chance that nothing would come of it. It would be disappointing, but Elizabeth did not want to allow herself to push aside the possibility.

That night, when the children were in tucked in bed and both were fast asleep, Elizabeth sat down at her desk to compose another letter to her suitor. She believed that she was passing the test so far, but she did not want to write anything that might make Frederick change his mind about her. She wanted to show him that she would be a good wife for him, and a good mother for his boys. Oh how she wished that she could go west with the letter to him and show him in person for herself. Words could only go so far in showing how a person truly was.

Dearest Mr. O'Connell,

Your letter reached me well and for that I am truly grateful. I wish however that my tidings about my life here were so good. Now that I am alone, I am burdened with the great responsibility of taking care of my home and my income all by myself. It is not something with which I wish to burden you, I only mention it because I know that it is something important that you must know. My situation of late has become dire and desperate.

Oh, do not for once think that it is the reason for my interest in receiving your letters. I must admit that it was the catalyst in my looking into the advertisements, but it was my heart which drew me to you. Surely you can understand.

Please do not be so frightfully hard on yourself about the choices you made in the past. My late husband fought valiantly, it is true, but he did not enjoy one moment of it and I'm sure you realize that I would have given anything to have stopped him from going to war.

I long for the adventure which you describe in your stories of your life out west. I long to run away someplace new and experience things I could never have imagined! It is my hope that someday, some way, I can find myself out there with you, exploring the plains and admiring the gold that is found in your mines.

You asked if I liked riding horses. It has been many years, as there is not much call for me to go off riding in the middle of a city, but of course I have been riding before. I would love to go riding with you on your ranch, if I may one day be so fortunate.

Warmest regards,

Elizabeth Beaumont

****

No letter or news came for several weeks. Elizabeth resumed her fretting about the rent and the other bills. One day, while the children were at school, she tearfully began packing up some things as though they were going to move somewhere else, but there was nowhere for them in Boston. There was nowhere for them anywhere.

The melancholy did not have long to control her thoughts, however. One unusually warm morning in late October, she received another letter from Frederick in California. The envelope also contained three train tickets!

Dear sweet Elizabeth,

When you wrote to me of your monetary woes, I had to do something. I hope that you will not think me forward, but I would very much like to have you and your children come to California and be with me. I have arranged for a nice hotel for you where you will be very comfortable and well looked after.

I look forward to making your acquaintance in person, and I hope we will soon be able to enjoy the much stronger bonds of friendship that can be shared when two friends live close together. All the best and I shall see you soon!

With sincerity,

Frederick

He had sent for her at last! He had not even employed his surname in the note – a clear sign of friendly, familial affection. He wanted her to be with him! Oh, Elizabeth felt as though she must be dreaming, but it was true. The letter was right there in her hands, along with the tickets.

It took approximately five weeks to reach California. Why, it would be December by the time they reached Frederick's ranch. Christmastime! She wondered how people celebrated Christmas in California. Did Frederick have a church that he went to for Mass? The children must go to Mass on Christmas. It was a tradition. The idea of going to a church in California was an exciting one. She knew that, even if it was different, it must not be far from the church she and her family was used to. They still prayed to the same God in California, to be sure.

As soon as the children came home from school, she just had to tell them the happy news. "Children," she said with a smile. "We are going on an adventure!"

"An adventure?!" Willie asked excitedly. He had a big imagination and loved going to visit new places, though he had never been outside of Massachusetts.

"Where are we going?" the more analytical Anne inquired. She enjoyed going to visit new places as well, but she was always a bit more wary of things that she had never experienced. She always wanted to know what the outcome would be, so she would know how to react.

Elizabeth held up the tickets so they could see. "We're going to California!" she said. "A very nice man has offered to let us live near him and spend time on his horse ranch. You like horses, don't you, Anne?"

Anne nodded eagerly at that. As she was a child of eight, horses were her favorite animal. She had been riding before, though fewer times than Elizabeth. Willie had only ever seen the horses pulling carriages and carts in the city. A horse ranch would be an entirely new experience for him.

Happy and filled with relief, Elizabeth packed the children's things into a suitcase before packing her own dresses and personal items. She thought better of trying to pack up all of her pots and housewares. The hotel most certainly would have such things and, if what Frederick said was true, their needs would be taken care of by the staff there. With any luck, the only time she would need to cook or clean again would be in considerate appreciation for Frederick's kind invitation.

The tickets were set for the first of November. As it was October 28th, they would have a few short days to remain in Boston and say their farewells to the things and people they held dear in that bustling city. As Frederick's children were ten and twelve years old, they most certainly went to a school of some sort. Anne and Willie would hopefully be able to attend with them.

There were so many things that Elizabeth was unsure about, but for the moment the not knowing was exciting to her. All of her life had been neatly written out for her until now. She hoped upon hope that, when they arrived in Douglas City, they would find the place to be as invigorating and satisfying as she had imagined.

The day arrived on which they were to depart. Willie took extra-long to tie his shoe laces, which Elizabeth attributed to nerves. Anne was struck by a sudden sadness and was crying as they made their way by carriage to the train station.

"Anne, whatever is the matter?" Elizabeth asked her, consoling her and hugging her close.

"I don't want to leave," Anne cried against her mother's shoulder. "I'm frightened of the train."

Elizabeth petted Anne's hair. Willie looked up at her with doleful eyes. The train loomed ahead of them, like a big, black monster in the eyes of the children. "Oh, don't be frightened, my loves," she said sweetly. "The train is going to take us to a magical new place. There are horses there, and a very nice man who will take care of all of us."

She was not sure how much more she should tell them about Frederick. She thought it best that, for now, he be presented simply as a benevolent fellow who had offered to help them. That way, an attachment to him could grow over time instead of them – especially Anne – feeling any resentment at their new father figure.

As she watched through the window as the trees and buildings of Massachusetts passed by, Elizabeth said a little prayer for her family. She said a prayer for Frederick and his family, too, and hoped that before too long their two families could become one.

Douglas City, California - 1866

The towns that came into view as the train came into northern California were ones made of dust and dirt, but the architecture was like nothing Elizabeth had ever seen before. Buildings were small and largely made of wooden planks. All the glamour of marble and stone had seemingly been left behind on the east coast. Anne was awake and looked out of the window with her, gaping in wonder at what she saw.

When the train pulled into the station, Elizabeth wondered how on earth she was going to find a carriage to bring them to Mr. O'Connell's provided lodgings. She had not been told that information. However, as she led one of the baggage attendants out of the train with her bags, she noticed someone was waving to her.

"Mrs. Beaumont!" the woman called. She was dressed in a nice, deep red dress, though the style was a bit more laid back than Elizabeth was accustomed to. Her white and black bodice was barely more than a jacket over her shoulders. She wore a straw hat with a black ribbon around the brim.

Elizabeth led her children by the hand over towards the mysterious woman, followed by the baggage attendant. "Yes?" she asked timidly. "I am Mrs. Beaumont."

The woman knowingly smiled at her. "I thought that was you. My name is Mrs. Davenport. Mr. O'Connell sent me along to fetch you from the station. He is awaiting your arrival at his home and would love to see you this evening for dinner there. Please, let me take you to the hotel and get you settled."

Mrs. Davenport had an accent that was like nothing else that Elizabeth had heard before. It was not quite as thick as the accents from the southern states, but it was not far off. She also spoke quickly and seemed to be sure of herself. Elizabeth wondered what her position was on Mr. O'Connell's ranch. She clearly worked for him in some capacity, to be shuttling his guests around.

The Beaumont family got into Mrs. Davenport's waiting carriage along with their bags. As promised, she had her driver take them straight to their new lodgings. It was a small but comfortable-looking hotel. As everything else in the town, it was built of wood and sandstone. The room they were assigned was a good size, with a small fireplace which might come in handy for the winter nights. One thing Elizabeth had noticed was that the temperatures in Douglas City were far different from the December temperatures of Boston. There was a slight nip in the air, but one could not truthfully call it cold. This was a relief to her, because she always worried about one or both of her children coming down with an illness during the winter months.

"I will let you all get settled now and come for you in about two hours for dinner with Mr. O'Connell," Mrs. Davenport said.

"Thank you, Mrs. Davenport," Elizabeth replied politely. "If I may ask, how are you acquainted with our host?" The older woman had the appearance of some sort of school teacher, though she was certainly a bit more lively and self-assured than the quiet, proper instructors Elizabeth had sent her children to.

Mrs. Davenport smiled kindly. "I am Mr. Connell's house keeper," she said. "Please, you may call me Amelia."

Elizabeth returned the smile. "It is so wonderful to meet you, Amelia. We will be ready when you return."

The housekeeper nodded respectfully and left the family to their business. Willie was sitting on his new bed, looking around the room in awe. Anne was still standing near the doorway, frowning.

"Take off your jacket, Anne," Elizabeth instructed. "Whatever are you frowning about? Don't you like your new home?"

"This isn't my new home," Anne replied, indignant. "This is a room."

Elizabeth went over to her and removed the jacket from the child's shoulders. "Yes, well, it's only our temporary home. We will get everything sorted out, and then we will have a nice, new house to live in. Won't you like that?"

She hoped that Frederick O'Connell would offer them the nice, new life that his advertisement and letters promised. She felt a bit uneasy and restless, now that they had made it all the way out to California. There was no turning back for them, and their lives depended on the man who was still essentially a stranger. What if he changed his mind and turned them away?

Elizabeth did her best not to think of it. She removed both children's jackets as well as her own, hanging them in the small closet that was provided to them. She tidied one of Willie's sleeves that was sagging over his hand. The clothing was still a bit too big on the five-year-old, but he would grow into them. Especially if he was well-fed, as she hoped he would be now.

Filling the wash basin, she gave the children each a quick bath, washing the dust from them and making them appear more presentable for their host. Mr. O'Connell had young children himself, so surely he would understand if her children were a bit dirty from the ride, but she had to do her best to keep them from looking entirely unkempt.

Before long, Mrs. Davenport – Amelia – arrived back at the hotel to accompany them to the house of the O'Connells. The carriage jostled them slightly along the dirt road, which did not help to calm Elizabeth's nerves. When they finally arrived at Mr. O'Connell's large ranch house, she looked down and noticed that one of her fingernails had been bitten down to nothing. She hoped that Frederick would not notice or, at the very least, would not mention it.

The family filed into the main sitting room of the house and sat together on a large, green, velvet sofa. The children both looked nervous, and Elizabeth looked around the ornately-decorated room, practically pinching herself to be sure that all of this was really happening to her. She had been so enamored with the idea of being rescued that she had forgotten the means with which she *was* being rescued. Gold had purchased this place. Gold had made all of this possible, and she was about to meet King Midas himself.

****

After several minutes that felt both like an eternity and no time at all, a door opened at the top of the long, spiraling staircase outside of the sitting room. Elizabeth looked up, gaping in curiosity, in time to see the man of the house emerge and come down the stairs.

He was taller than she had anticipated, with copper hair that shined in the light of the sun coming in through the tall windows in the hall. He wore a stylish cream and orange colored suit, with an orange ascot around his neck. He looked more like a gentleman than any sort of cowboy she had heard of, but that suited her just as well. She was not sure how she should converse with a cowboy.

As he came closer, she could see his eyes. They were very kind, and they sparkled like emeralds. She had not anticipated him having green eyes. Richard had had green eyes, though his had been a darker shade. Still, the fact that Frederick had such dazzling, familiar eyes made her smile and almost become emotional.

"Welcome," he said in a friendly, cheerful voice. "You must be Mrs. Beaumont. It gives me great pleasure to have you here." Bowing, he took her hand and gave it a kiss. His mustache tickled, and she smiled at him, blushing profusely.

"I'm pleased to make your acquaintance at long last, Mr. O'Connell," she said, giving him a small curtsy.

He laughed brightly, shaking his head a bit. "No need to curtsy, Mrs. Beaumont. The honor is all mine. And please, call me Frederick. We are friends, aren't we?"

She smiled, blushing even more. "Yes," she said. "Oh, yes, I hope so. Please call me Elizabeth. And these are my children." She gestured for her children to come over, and they stood on either side of her, staying close to her skirts. "This is Anne, and this is Willie."

Frederick's smile only grew bigger at the sight of the little ones. He leaned down so he could greet them more at their level. "How do you do?" he said, nodding his head politely at them.

"How do you do?" they both murmured in response, shy.

He raised himself back up to his full height. "Well, there is some time before dinner will be fully prepared. Stephen and Davy are outside, riding their horses, if you children would like to go meet them."

Willie's face lit up at the prospect of meeting two new little boys who were around his age. "Oh yes, can we, Mama?"

Elizabeth nodded happily. This was indeed one of the reasons she had reached out to Frederick in the first place. He led them outside to his stables and the running field beyond it. Two little boys, aged ten and twelve, were riding around on brown and white horses.

Anne finally smiled when she saw the horses. "Oh, Mommy, can I ride a horse, too?" she asked excitedly.

"I can start teaching you how to ride them, if you'd like," Frederick said, looking over at Elizabeth for approval. "These horses are young, so they might be a bit more temperamental than you're used to."

Anne looked over at Elizabeth as well, pleading with her big blue eyes.

Elizabeth laughed. "Well, I think that will be nice," she said. "But you'll have to go slowly, Anne. And be sure to listen to what Mr. O'Connell tells you."

Frederick whistled for his sons. "Boys, come over here! I need to introduce you."

The two O'Connell boys dismounted from their horses and sent them into the stables before coming over. They were dusty from the ride, and Elizabeth smiled to herself. She had been worried about her kids being dirty.

"Stephen, David, this is Mrs. Elizabeth Beaumont and her children. Anne, Willie, these are my sons."

Everyone said hello to each other. The two boys looked very much like their father, though they had blue eyes that Elizabeth surmised they got from their mother. Stephen, the elder boy, was already quite tall for his age. He wore his long, red hair in a ponytail, making him look like a young Thomas Jefferson. Davy, the younger boy, was wearing a cowboy hat that was about two sizes too big for his head.

Stephen leaned over and whispered something to Davy, which caused his little brother to laugh loudly.

Elizabeth smiled at them, keen to be friends. "What's so funny?" she asked.

"You all look like city slickers," Davy blurted, laughing even more. Stephen laughed at him for saying it out loud.

Anne frowned at them. "What does that mean?"

"It means you look like you've never seen a farm before, or a horse," Stephen explained in a none-too-friendly tone.

Elizabeth's eyes widened and she looked at Frederick for help. He shook his head. "Boys, don't be rude. They came all the way from Boston at my request."

That only caused them to cackle further. "Why did you send for a teacher all the way from Boston?" Stephen asked. "We're happy with Miss Turner. She understands us better than Mrs. Beaumont could."

Frederick sighed and looked slightly embarrassed. "Boys, I did not invite Elizabeth here to be your new teacher. I invited her here because she is my friend."

The boys stopped laughing and Stephen fixed his father with a hurt, icy stare. "We don't need a new mother either."

Gesturing to Davy, Stephen turned on his heel and the brothers went back to their horses that were waiting for them in the stable.

Elizabeth looked down at the ground. Her face was flushed, for a different reason now. She had not anticipated this reaction from Frederick's sons. From the look on his face, neither had he.

The first dinner with the O'Connells passed mostly in awkward silence. Frederick did his best to be the jovial host, telling Elizabeth stories about his gold discoveries and his plans for the ranch. She smiled at him, but it was difficult to feel any sort of bond with him at present. His children's icy attitudes had not helped. Nor did it help that those same children were at the table with them, along with her own children. It was hard to get any sense of how he felt, because they could not be quite so frank with the young people around them on all sides.

Thankfully, after dinner, Mrs. Davenport offered to watch the children while Elizabeth and Frederick took some time to get to know one another better. "Leave them with me, Mrs. Beaumont," she said with a friendly wink. "I'll get those children to behave whether they like it or not."

Elizabeth thanked her and Amelia shooed her out of the living room to the hallway, where Frederick was waiting for her. He offered his arm and Elizabeth gladly took it. No matter how his children were, at least Frederick was still a gentleman.

They walked together along the front path of his ranch, past his pastures and barns and stables. She was quite fond of the fact that he had used his money to build a nice home for his family that was both cozy and, to her mind, uniquely Californian. For a few moments, no words passed between them, though they were both pleased to be in each other's company.

Finally, Frederick broke the silence. "I hope that you like it here, Mrs. Beaumont—Elizabeth. I apologize for the way my boys acted today. They are not usually like that, but...well, I suppose you can understand that they have taken the death of Charlotte pretty hard. They didn't always behave for her, either, but she was their mother and they loved her very much."

Elizabeth nodded. Of course she understood. "I do," she said. "I don't expect them to be completely ready for changes so suddenly. Why, my children and even I are not quite used to everything here yet. Things like this take time, I only hope that, in the end, they can accept me as part of their family. *Your* family." She looked over at him and smiled, blushing a little.

Frederick smiled back at her appreciatively. "I am glad to hear you say that and I agree with you completely. Everything new takes a little time."

When they had finished their walk, they stood together on the front porch a moment before going back inside. He looked like he wanted to say something to her, but held back. He reached out and gently touched her cheek, causing her to blush anew.

"Good night, darling," he said to her sweetly. "I hope we shall do this again tomorrow. Hopefully with better-behaved children."

Elizabeth bid him good night and thanked him for their dinner. Then, she gathered up her two sleepy children and climbed into the coach that would take them to back to their hotel for the night.

"She's a nice lady," Mrs. Davenport told Frederick as soon as the Beaumonts were gone.

"Yes," Mr. O'Connell replied. "I think so, too."

****

The following day at the ranch, the children were disappointingly worse. Stephen and Anne bickered about who got to ride the horses and Davy and Willie nearly came to blows over some other silly thing. Despite Elizabeth and Frederick's best efforts, they could not get them to settle down for their day together. Elizabeth's frustration grew until ultimately she made the decision to gather up Anne and Willie and retreat to the hotel for dinner.

"Why can't you get along?" Elizabeth asked them, frustrated and embarrassed. "Mr. O'Connell is my new friend, and you two can't be nice and let us be together."

"Davy said that you're going to be their mommy, too," Willie said with a pout. "You're *our* mommy, not theirs."

Understanding, Elizabeth brought Willie into her lap, smoothing back some wayward hair from his face. "I will always be your mommy," she said. "But Stephen and Davy lost their mother. Just like you and your sister lost your daddy." She bit her lip to keep it from trembling. She missed Richard. He was always more adept at reasoning with the children. Perhaps because he understood the way they thought. She did her best at being a single mother, but knew in her heart that both she and the children longed for something more.

"I want us all to be a family," she said, looking from Willie to Anne. "Don't you think that would be nice? You would have a new father. He won't replace your daddy, but he will be there for you, and love you. Don't you want that?"

The children looked down guiltily and nodded.

"Sorry, Mama," Anne said. "I just don't like Stephen!"

Elizabeth chuckled softly. "Well, not yet. But you don't have to like someone in order to get along with them. Just be nice to both of them and see what happens. Okay?"

Her children nodded. They were still so young and eager to make her happy. She hoped that Frederick's boys could be the same way towards him.

They gave a lunchtime get together another try the following day. It was beginning to get chillier outside as Christmastime was in the air. Elizabeth wore a nice, red dress to be more into the spirit, and Anne was wearing a green velvet dress. Willie was dressed in a smart little suit. It was a Sunday lunch, and Elizabeth was hoping that the O'Connell brood could be persuaded to go to church with them after the meal. It would be a good way to test the waters before Christmas, and predict what the holiday might be like for the two families.

"Oh," Frederick said, a look of concern on his face. "The boys haven't been to church since their mother died." He and Elizabeth were speaking together in hushed tones while the children were yammering to each other in – so far – polite bursts of conversation.

Elizabeth felt a bit disappointed, but she could understand. Funerals could shake a person's trust in God, especially if that person was so young. "Then may we come back after church for dinner? Today seems to be a fine day for visiting." She nodded towards the children to emphasize her point.

Frederick smiled and nodded. "I would be delighted to see you again later."

Just then, Stephen stood up, stamping his foot and glaring angrily at Anne. "You will not be riding my horse! I won't let you!"

Oh dear, Elizabeth thought. *Not again.*

"I don't want to ride *your* horse. I want to ride one of Mr. O'Connell's horses!" Anne cried.

"The O'Connell horses *are my horses*!" Stephen shot back.

"Enough!" Frederick yelled. "Enough, both of you. If you can't behave, no one will be riding horses again. Is that understood?"

The children all mumbled their assent.

Frederick narrowed his eyes a bit, looking at Stephen. "Now, Mrs. Beaumont has invited us to go along to church with her. I think it's high time you two went back to reading the Bible. We're going to go." He looked at Elizabeth. "It is clear that they could use a few lessons."

She smiled at him, pleased to see that the outburst had changed his mind.

Despite being long removed from church-going, Stephen and David did better than Elizabeth could have imagined when they all went together to the small Douglas City chapel. They already dressed nicely, but they cleaned up exceedingly well when they were away from the horses and dust.

"*My little children*," they all read in unison with the priest. "*Let us not love in word, neither in tongue; but in deed and in truth.*"

After going to the church, the children's spirits seemed to be lifted. Anne babbled to Davy about how long they had been riding horses. It made Elizabeth happy to see peace restored to them.

Dinner was enjoyed with much pleasanter discussion. Frederick was gifted at story-telling and told them all about a baby cow he had once rescued from falling into a mine. He had the children laughing together and it seemed that everything would be all right at last.

"Mama," Anne told her excitedly as Elizabeth tucked her into bed that night. "I'm going to ride a horse tomorrow!"

Elizabeth smiled at her. "Oh, that will be nice. But you must promise me that you will be patient and listen to what Mr. O'Connell tells you. And no more fighting with Stephen."

Anne shook her head. "I won't fight with him anymore. As long as he doesn't fight with me."

Elizabeth laughed lightly. She admired her little girl's spirit. She had always been shyer than Anne ever was. Willie had inherited Elizabeth's quieter demeanor. She supposed that Anne was a product of her soldier father's personality. That suited her just fine.

The trouble with Anne's fiery personality was that, sometimes, she would promise one thing but then go ahead and do whatever was in her head instead.

The following day, at the stables, Anne complained loud enough and long enough that she finally was able to sit on the taller of the two horses that were offered.

"Brawny is not afraid to throw anybody," Stephen cautioned from the fence. "He's even almost thrown my dad before. So be careful."

In the holiday spirit, Elizabeth had Anne dress in another Christmas dress. Although the little girl was excited about the day's riding session, Elizabeth hoped that it would not be too long and it would not result in any stains or rips in the nice dress.

"Watch me, Mama!" Anne called from horseback. She kicked the heels of her small boots into the horse's sides and Brawny took off like a shot.

No one was expecting him to do that, least of all Anne. She let out a frightened scream, holding on for dear life.

"Aw, heck," Frederick said, panicked.

Stephen swung himself over the fence and rushed into the stables to fetch Brainy, the smaller but no less tough other horse. He quickly clambered onto the horse's back and took off after Brawny and Anne.

Elizabeth felt herself swooning as she watched her poor child screaming and racing around the field. Frederick caught her before she could fall and held her in his arms. "Elizabeth, I am so sorry. Don't worry, watch and wait, Stephen will help her."

Stephen did just that. His horse caught up with Brawny and he was able to carefully pull her off of the wild horse's back. He held onto her with one hand and grabbed Brawny's reigns with the other, forcing him to stop and stand still.

Frederick pointed, smiling. "See? She's all right, Elizabeth."

Elizabeth opened her eyes and looked over, smiling in relief.

He was so happy to see that she was all right that he kissed her, a light little peck on her lips.

Elizabeth blushed at him, looking him the emerald eyes. "You're going to make me faint again."

"I will buy her a pony," Frederick said. "A sweet little pony that won't pull stunts like that." He looked Elizabeth in the eyes lovingly.

Stephen helped Anne down from the back of Brainy. "Are you all right?"

Anne nodded, still a bit shaken but in one piece. "Thank you…" she said softly.

He smiled at her and gave the little girl's back a gentle pat. "I didn't want you to get hurt," he said.

"Mrs. Beaumont," Frederick asked, taking Elizabeth's soft little hand in his large, rough one. "I know that there is still much to do and our children still need to come together more, but it appears that they're well on their way now. Would you do me the honor of becoming Mrs. O'Connell on Christmas?"

Elizabeth fanned herself with her other hand. Tears filled her eyes. This was what she had come for and what she had needed and wanted. It has been assumed that he would marry her, but now that he had officially asked, she was free to show all of her happiness and thrill at the prospect.

"Yes, Mr. O'Connell," she said, adopting his formal name since he had used hers. "I would be delighted."

****

The wedding took place in the small chapel that Elizabeth had found for the family. She was dressed all in white and lace, with a long veil and a dress train that went on behind her for what seemed like miles.

Anne and Willie were dressed to the nines, too, and they seemed happy that their mother was marrying her friend who they were quickly growing to adore. Even Stephen and Davy had finally come around and were pleased to see that their father was happy with someone again.

Before the ceremony began, Elizabeth thoughtfully pulled off the wedding ring that Richard had given her. She kissed it and moved it to the ring finger on her right hand. "I love you, Richard," she whispered, wondering if he could hear her from Heaven above.

She had made the decision to marry Frederick before she had truly met him, but now that she had spent a few weeks with him, she could tell without a doubt that they would be quite happy together. Their children would be untroubled, too and she could see strong bonds quickly forming between her children and Frederick's. Together, they would all be one big happy family.

During the ceremony, she kept her eyes on Frederick, who continued to look over and smile reassuringly at her. His copper hair shined brilliantly in the light of the candles in the church and he looked every bit the handsome knight that she dreamed he would be. She knew that, whatever trials they may face together in the future, that he would be by her side and that they would weather any storm together with ease.

"Elizabeth," said the priest. "Do you take Frederick to be your husband, to have and to hold, to honor and to obey, to love and to cherish as long as you both shall live?"

She smiled at Frederick. The things she had heard about the mail order bride service were not entirely true in her case, she believed. She was not marrying a stranger. She was marrying a friend. A friend that she had come to love dearly.

"I do," she said as she smiled at him.

The priest asked the same thing of Frederick and received the same response. "I now pronounce you man and wife," he finally announced. "You may kiss the bride."

Elizabeth blushed as Frederick leaned in to her, smiling sweetly. "I love you, Lizzie," he said.

The nickname melted her heart. "I love you too, Freddie," she said in response, giggling softly.

He wrapped his arms around her and held her close, kissing her sweetly as everyone at the wedding cheered.

Afterwards, when they emerged from the chapel they were pleasantly surprised to find a thin layer of snow on the ground. "How beautiful! I didn't know it snowed in California! What a lovely gift on our wedding day." Elizabeth said in surprise.

Frederick softly chuckled "Perhaps it's the Lord's way of agreeing that our union is extra special. That's what I'd like to think. Would you agree, Darling?"

She did, and so did the children, who immediately started playing in it – all four of them, together.

ABIGAIL'S CHRISTMAS GIFT

New York, 1870

Abigail Copeland's life in New York City was beginning to stagnate. She enjoyed her life as a nurse, helping to care for the wounded and sick that came into the hospital's doors. She was a nurturing mother figure, though she had no husband or family of her own. The influx of people coming into the city from other countries brought along all sorts of things, including extra patients for her to care for. They told her stories of their homelands and all of the things that they had been glad to leave behind. These immigrants brought something else with them, too: they awoke in Abigail a desire to explore new territories and experience more of what life had to offer her.

"You don't need to go anywhere," her mother Helen told her. "This town is as good a town as any to make a living and raise a family. What you need is to find a good man who will take care of you."

Abigail's mother was ever the traditionalist. She wanted to see her pretty daughter married off to the first well-to-do man who offered. It was not for lack of trying that Abigail did not have a husband or a beau by now. The men who were around her were largely already married or in some way undesirable. Marrying someone who was never going to be around for her seemed no better than not marrying at all. She had a sneaking suspicion that her mother wanted her to marry one of the patients at the hospital. Abigail did not want to marry someone who was sick and might possibly die. She wanted to marry someone strong and different from the New York men she was so used to.

When the weather turned colder and Abigail and Helen were huddled close to their fireplace for warmth, the newspaper became rather inviting. Abigail opened it up to the page of advertisements for brides and female companions. She curiously read over several of the letters. The one that stood out to her the most was from a gentleman named Samuel Merriweather who lived in Coos Bay, Oregon. One of the first things that drew her to him was how young he was.

"Gentleman widower, 33 years of age, 6 feet tall and handsome hoping to find a kind young woman who will love and care for him as well as his child."

Abigail appreciated the man's emphasis on kindness. So many of the other ads demanded photographs. Mr. Merriweather's advertisement included a small portrait of him. He was surely handsome, with long, dark hair and a haunting expression. He was dressed differently from any man she had ever seen, with a floppy hat and suspenders in place of the fancy suits and cravats she was used to seeing the eligible men wear in New York. It made her sad that someone so young was already a widower.

Her mother was nodding off, enjoying the heat of the fire, and Abigail took the opportunity to write a quick letter in response to this Samuel Merriweather.

Dear Mr. Merriweather,

I was captivated by your advertisement and thought that I must write to you promptly. My name is Abigail Copeland and I am a single maid, working as a nurse in New York City. I am twenty-five years old and I live alone with my mother, who is a widow. My father passed away in the War.

I have often dreamt of what the West must be like. I envision rolling hills and sunshine and cows. The only western experience I have at this point comes from stories I have heard from some of my patients, though I do not know if they are truthful or not. Is it really as wonderful as it seems?

I have enclosed a few photographs of myself so that you may trust that I am as I have described.

I would love it ever so much if I could join you out West this Christmas and help to bring joy back to the lives of you and your son again.

Please write back to me. I hope to hear more from you and would much appreciate the chance to get to know you better.

Sincerely,

Miss Abigail Copeland

Once her letter was completed and tucked carefully away into an envelope, Abigail added two or three photographs to serve as evidence that she really was as she said. In one of the photographs, she was wearing her nurse's uniform, tending to the needs of a sickly young man. She had slightly curly, dark red tresses that she kept long though usually tied back while she was working. Her blue eyes were vaguely cat-like and her skin was like cream. She hoped that Mr. Merriweather would find her looks appealing and would write back to her in confidence.

Helen awoke from her napping to find Abigail in the process of closing up the envelope. She looked from Abigail to the open newspaper page and smiled knowingly at her. "Are you heeding my advice?" she asked happily. "Are you finally seeking a husband?"

Abigail pouted slightly. She did not like how vulgar that sounded. She was not writing to Mr. Merriweather merely to marry herself off. She was writing to him because she cared enough to know more about him, in the hopes of creating a friendship. "I am seeking to help someone," she said.

Her mother continued to smile. "If he is rich, why should he need help?"

Abigail sighed. Her mother was a good person; she just clung to the old fashioned opinion that wealth was all it took to make someone prosperous. Abigail, conversely, believed that love, passion and adventure were important in order to achieve true happiness.

Love, passion and adventure were things that she did not believe she would be able to find in her native New York. She felt the call to go west and make so much more for herself. Love, passion and adventure…those were the sorts of things that she hoped awaited her in Coos Bay, Oregon.

****

One of Abigail's dear patients that she had been nursing for several weeks died unexpectedly in the night. Though she told herself that she should be used to such things by now, she couldn't manage to hold the tears back. It was never easy to lose someone. She blamed herself. "I should have been there," she cried to the doctor who had been tending to him.

"Nonsense," the kind hearted man told her. "Miss Copeland, you did your best. No one can expect you to be here at all hours of the day and night." He gave her shoulder a gentle pat. "Go home and get some rest."

When she arrived home, weary and heartbroken, her mother handed her an envelope with Coos Bay inscribed on it in neat cursive handwriting. "This should cheer you up," Helen said, though she had no idea what the response might actually say.

Abigail pulled off her nurse's cap and set it aside on the table, bringing the letter into her lap and carefully opened the envelope. She marveled a bit at the handwriting, wondering how he had come to write so neatly.

My dear Miss Copeland,

Your kind response to my advertisement has filled my heart with great joy. To know that a woman with such beauty could ever care about me and my plight gives me relief and helps to lift my spirits in my troubled time of need.

As you know from my description, my wife has died. She passed on from Tuberculosis early in this year and left me with a son, 5 years old. He is a wonderful child, smart and polite, but he has become sickly and I do not know how to take care of him on my own.

It is a comfort to me to know that you are a nurse. Perhaps you might do me the honor of joining us in our home and helping me to care for my son. Your mother is welcome to join us as well. I believe that you would find Coos Bay to be a most exciting and lively town. It is surely quite different from New York, but perhaps that would not be a bad thing for you.

What a wonderful Christmas present it would be for us both, to have you here!

I look forward to your response and I hope that it might include a 'yes' to my invitation.

All the best,

Mr. Samuel Merriweather

Abigail found herself smiling and blushing at Mr. Merriweather's letter. She had not expected him to be so welcoming towards both her and her mother. Somehow, he seemed to understand that the hustle and bustle of New York had grown stale to her. And his poor son! Could it be that his son had come down with Tuberculosis as well? She hoped not. Even if she went to them at once, she most likely would not be able to cure him of an illness that was so grave.

"It seems that, no matter where I go, I am to be surrounded by sickness and death," she sadly confessed to her mother.

Helen shook her head, taking the letter so she could read it over herself. "He wants us there already?" she asked, excitement plainly showing on her face.

Abigail nodded. Though she was excited at the prospect of being invited to journey west, she was a bit saddened by the idea that she was going there to act as nurse for a sick child. Still, the fact that she was needed appealed to her helpful, nurturing personality. She was not simply being called upon to act as an attractive accessory; she was going to be aiding a family that was still mourning the loss of its matriarch. Abigail wondered, dreamily, if she was going to be asked to be the new matriarch of the small Merriweather family. She imagined herself as the head of their household, caring for the sick young Merriweather child while simultaneously bouncing a new baby on her hip. It was certainly not the sort of thing she had aspired to be, but as she aged she could feel the undeniable pull of motherhood.

Mr. Merriweather and his son needed her.

Taking up her pen and paper, she wrote a letter in response.

Dearest Mr. Merriweather,

My mother and I are pleased to accept your invitation to join you at your home in Coos Bay, Oregon. I only hope that we will arrive there in time to make sure that your son receives the proper care that he needs.

I cannot imagine what Christmas must be like there. Here, we have department stores that become decorated overnight as if by elves, and everyone goes around to explore them as if they were not just places of business but wondrous sites to see! Christmas must be much more calm and focused on family out West, is it not? After spending many a holiday in New York, I am more than ready to experience something new in someplace far different. As an outsider, I will do my utmost to make it the most wonderful day for you both.

Fondest regards,

Abigail Copeland

Waiting for a response was agonizing for her. Every day that went by made her fret that something terrible had happened to the little boy, or that Samuel had changed his mind about the whole thing. She wished that she had been able to grow wings, so that she may arrive in Oregon sooner.

Her boss, Miss Dowdy, the head nurse at the hospital, was sad to hear that Abigail would soon be leaving. "You will be greatly missed," she said. "But how delightful that you shall be exploring out West. I do hope that you will keep in touch."

"I will keep in touch," Abigail promised her. "In fact, I may need your assistance in caring for this sick child. You are one of the greatest practitioners I know."

She was not sure how much the nurse would be able to assist with caring for the child, but she knew that it was always wise to accept help when it was offered. Until she met the little boy, she was not entirely sure that she would be of much help to him either. Oh, but she hoped so…

Finally, after several weeks of worrying and wringing her hands in anxiousness, a new letter arrived from Samuel Merriweather.

My dear Miss Copeland,

I was deeply relieved to read that you would like to come to Oregon and be with us. As you say, time is of the essence. I have enclosed two tickets to a ship that will bring you from New York to Coos Bay, by way of Boston and San Francisco.

Christmas will be all the more wonderful simply for having you here with me. You tell such lovely stories. I have told my son your story of the decorated stores and he has requested going to see them in person. Perhaps someday, when you are longing to visit your hometown again, we can see these visions for ourselves. I do not doubt that yours will be a most beloved presence here this holiday season.

I pray that you will have a safe journey and I will do my best to be sure that I am there when you arrive.

All the best,
Samuel Merriweather

****

Mrs. Helen Copeland would not be moved as easily as Abigail. When she was told that Mr. Merriweather had sent along some boat tickets for them and that they were expected to move to Oregon, she looked as though she had swallowed a mouse.

"Are you sure this is a good idea?" she asked Abigail. "Moving all the way over there for some stranger?"

Abigail smiled slightly at her. "It is something that a lot of young women are doing these days. You wanted me to get married. I don't see why this way is not a perfect way to go about it. I will even be able to continue my occupation!"

Maintaining at least some semblance of her nursing career was something that Abigail really hoped she would be able to achieve. If men could be married while still being able to pursue careers, why couldn't a woman? And, after all, Mr. Merriweather highly prized Abigail's abilities as a nurse. He surely would let her continue to use her skills, once his son was better.

Oh, she hoped she would be able to make his son better! How dreadful it would be to go all the way there on that promise, only for the little boy to die…

Abigail and her mother packed up their things, careful to remember that they must pack up everything because they would not be coming back. It was hard for Helen to fathom at first, so Abigail did her best to rouse some excitement out of her. "We're going to explore the open country," she told her. "Think of all the things we shall see! Why, we may even stumble upon something that no one has discovered yet. Won't that be amazing?"

Her mother smiled slightly at her. "I've seen enough of the world to be satisfied," she replied. "But if I see you married there, that will make *me* happy. Is this man terribly rich?"

"Oh, obscenely," Abigail said. She actually had no idea; it was merely an assumption. One could not buy an ad in the newspaper without a decent bit of money and she thought that, as a coal miner in Coos Bay, he must surely have a lot of money by now. The miners out there had been a great success, according to the newspapers and word on the streets. She wondered if he had mined any gold.

"Good," her mother said. "I want to see you married well. I married well and never wanted for a thing…until your father passed away." She suddenly looked sad. "Now I would trade everything to get him back."

Abigail gently laid a hand on her mother's shoulder.

"That is the sort of marriage I want for you," Helen said at last, shaking away the sadness and carrying on with her packing. "I hope this Samuel Merriweather can give you that and he does not expect you to be his glorified wet nurse."

Abigail blushed. "Mother! It is not like that. Besides, I am quite sure the boy has been looked after by doctors there as well. It is just a convenience that I have nursing skills. If he had intended for his advertisement to be for simply a nurse, he would have said so."

She wanted to believe that. After all, he had called her lovely. What did it matter if a nurse was lovely?

Once all of their things were packed up to be sent off on a train, they were ready for their boat ride. At least, Abigail was. "I've never been on a boat before," her mother said, wringing her hands nervously on the train on the way to Boston. "What if I get sick?"

"I'll be with you, Mother," Abigail replied soothingly. "If you get sick, I will take care of you. But I don't think you will get sick. Remember, I've never been on a boat either and I am not worried about it in the least."

"That's because you are young," Helen said with a slight wink. "Young people are not afraid of anything. At least, they shouldn't be."

The train ride was long enough that the two women were asleep by the time they arrived in Boston. Then they groggily boarded their ship to San Francisco, not looking forward to the fact that it would take an additional train ride afterward to get them to Coos Bay. It was quite a lot of travel to get from point A to point B.

Abigail was amused to discover that the ship was largely heralded as a "mail order bride" ship. Many of the passengers were well-dressed young women around her age. Most of them, like her, had a chaperone such as a mother or perhaps an elder sister. She wondered what sort of things might go on with these strange men, if chaperones were needed.

Finding some alone time on the boat, Abigail longed to be able to speak with Samuel. She could not even write to him now. She wondered, languidly, what his life was like and what his little boy was like.

The sea stretched on ahead, and although she did not feel sick on the ship, she hoped that she might never need to make a journey like this again. She wanted desperately to feel as though she belonged somewhere and was needed.

When they docked at last in San Francisco, California, Abigail and her mother took in as many of the sights as they could before and while on their final leg of their journey. The west was as beautiful and different as Abigail had hoped. She wished that she could stop in and see what it was like in the mines, but she knew that she would be shooed away immediately. Mines were men's work. She did not want to get dirty, but she certainly was curious to see what sort of things went into mining. Perhaps her new husband would show her.

Oh! Her new husband! She had not really thought of Samuel in that way yet. She had spent so long fretting about how she might help him that she had not fully realized that he was going to be her husband. They would be able to help each other. The thought excited her, and she also grew nervous at the prospect of meeting him. What if he did not find her as attractive as he had desired? What if he was disappointed in her? What if *she* was disappointed in *him*? She knew that she did not have a say in the matter, but she hoped that she could be happy with him. After all, they would be living together…

After a while, all of the west outside of her window started to appear the same, much like the east did to her mind. The invisible boundaries of the states were not apparent at all, and she wondered aloud if they were anywhere near Oregon yet.

"Yes, Miss," a friendly coachman told her, chuckling. "We're coming up on Coos Bay next."

"Oh that's marvelous," Abigail said. "Did you hear that, Mother?" She nudged her mother awake. "We're nearly there!"

Dear Mr. Merriweather, she thought. *We are almost to your home and so anxious to meet you at last. I pray that your little one is safe.*

She hoped that she would be everything that Samuel dreamed she would be, and she prayed that he would be everything she had hoped for as well.

Coos Bay, Oregon 1870

Once their train had stopped at the station and the attendant had helped them with their luggage, Abigail and Helen Copeland stood on the platform, looking around in wonder and no small bit of trepidation.

There was no sign of the man they had come to see. No one held up a sign with their names on it, or even asked them where they were trying to go. Now that they had arrived, Abigail had no idea what they should do next.

December in Oregon was not a good time for standing out in the drafts. Abigail wrapped her coat around herself and led her mother out to the dirt-filled road. She waved her hands at the passing carriages until she finally got one to stop. "Please sir," she beseeched. "We have just arrived in town. Could you tell us how to get to—" She pulled out one of Samuel's envelopes. "—One eleven Hickory Road?"

The driver of the carriage considered it a moment. "I think I know how to get thereabouts," he replied. He helped her and Helen with their suitcases and then helped them to climb aboard his coach.

"Thank you so much," Abigail said sincerely. "Someone was meant to pick us up at the station, but he did not appear."

"If the person who was supposed to get you was Mr. Samuel Merriweather, I should not be surprised why he did not show up," the kind driver said, shaking the reins and sending his horses off on a trot. "His boy is terribly ill. Has been for quite some time."

Abigail frowned, feeling dreadful for wondering at their greeter's tardiness. If Samuel had meant to be the one to greet them upon their arrival, then it was no wonder that he had been unable to be there. He should not leave his son unattended, especially if the situation was dire.

"Is he very ill?" she asked in a sympathetic tone, as though the man must surely know everything about it.

The driver shook his head a little, appearing sad himself. "I don't know the Merriweathers all that well," he said. "But the word about town is that the little fellow is always sick with something. Ever since his mother died."

Abigail frowned. "Oh, that's awful," she said. "Oh, I hope I'm not too late."

"Too late?" he asked. "Are you a doctor?" He looked at her, seeming to appraise her looks for a moment. "You're from New England, aren't you? They have women doctors there now?"

Abigail straightened up in her seat, feeling slightly offended. "They have had women doctors in the northeast for quite some time. I am, however, a nurse. I believe I may be of some help to Mr. Merriweather's child."

The driver slowly smiled at her. "Indeed you will be. I think you'll be of great help to Mr. Merriweather, too."

She rode the rest of the way in silence, her head spinning slightly as she thought about what this driver had said. Could she really be of great help to Mr. Merriweather? Oh, she hoped so!

****

The house that the carriage stopped in front of was large and solemn-looking. A large, black wreath that signified mourning was on the front door. Abigail wondered if the people inside were still deep in mourning. Was it right to come into their lives and assume the position of matriarch? Samuel was clearly hoping for such a thing, but it made her feel odd. Possibly the little boy would feel the same way about all of this.

Abigail and Helen thanked the man for driving them to the house and alit from the carriage, carefully carrying their bags up to the front door with them. Abigail knocked, feeling a sense of dread as though she might possibly be intruding on a funeral.

A middle-aged woman answered the door. She was dressed in a moss green dress, with an apron and a white bonnet. "Hello?" she asked, before smiling at the newcomers. "You must be Miss Copeland. Mr. Merriweather told me to expect you any day now. Please come in."

She held the door open for Abigail and her mother. They stepped inside and another servant swiftly took their bags away to another room.

"Please let me help you with your coats," the woman who greeted them said. "You must be tired from your travels. My name is Mrs. Bertha Mills. You can call me Bertha. Mr. Merriweather is in town at the moment, picking up some things at the drug store. Would you like me to see you to your rooms?"

Helen and Abigail looked at each other. "Thank you very much for your hospitality, Bertha. Please call me Abigail. This is my mother, Mrs. Helen Copeland…if you please, may I have a glass of water. I am a bit too restless at the moment to go to my room." She smiled at the housekeeper – for that was clearly Bertha's position – and hoped that it was not to presumptuous of her to stay out in the sitting room.

Her mother, on the other hand, happily went off to see her new room. The trip had been more tiresome for the older woman. Indeed, she had much less to be excited about whereas Abigail's nerves were buzzing with the excitement – and a little bit of fear – at meeting the man that she was to marry.

As Bertha showed Helen to her room, Abigail explored around the sitting room of Mr. Merriweather's house. On the wall, with a black drapery around it, was a portrait of a beautiful young woman that could only be his late wife. Abigail's heart ached for Samuel. To have lost someone so young, and now be worried for the health of their child…it was enough to break anyone's heart.

Just as she was standing there looking at the portrait, Bertha came back into the room with a glass of water for Abigail. She saw that the young woman was admiring the painting and let out a sad little sigh. "It has not been the same around here," she said, slightly startling Abigail who had not noticed that she had returned.

"No, I imagine not," Abigail replied with a sadness of her own. She gratefully accepted the offered glass of water and took a long sip from it. The journey west had made her mighty thirsty and she did not want to start feeling sickly. That would be the last thing Samuel would want or need more of.

Abigail sat upon one of the sofas in the sitting room, continuing to admire the paintings on the walls as well as the books on the shelves. She heard the sound of the front door opening and straightened up in her seat, almost as though she had been doing something wrong.

"Bertha!" a young man's voice called from the foyer. It was not too deep, and it was bright-sounding which surprised Abigail due to the sadness that surrounded the place.

She did not have long to wonder about his voice however, because a few moments later he stepped into the sitting room. He was tall, with dark hair that curled a bit as it brushed against his shoulders. His eyes were a piercing blue, and he had the beginnings of a beard and mustache, most likely from being too busy caring for his son to worry about shaving.

Abigail stood up at once from her position on the sofa and gave a polite bow. "Hello, Mr. Merriweather."

He suddenly stared at her, and she felt her heart swell in her chest. He was ever so handsome! And he did not look like anyone she had ever seen in New York, except perhaps an immigrant which made her even more excited.

"Why, Miss Copeland," he said, giving her a small smile and taking her hand in his. "How wonderful to have you here at last." He gave her hand a kiss and she blushed shyly.

He looked around for Bertha and, not finding his maid about, he returned to Abigail. He gestured for her to sit back down and he sat beside her, careful to keep a cushion between them.

"Have you been here long?" he asked her pleasantly. "Has Bertha gone to fetch Tommy for you yet?"

"Oh, no," Abigail said, shaking her head. She did not know who Tommy was, but she could guess. "Bertha was just here with me so she cannot have gone far."

The maid was awfully good at quietly slipping to and from the rooms of the house. Abigail thought that it must largely be due to the fact that the sick Tommy needed quiet.

"Oh," Samuel replied. She wondered if she was allowed to call him Samuel. She would have to ask, later when he was not quite so frantic. "Well, no matter. I will go get Tommy from his bedchamber so you can see him. Would you like that?"

Abigail did not really want the young man to leave again so soon, for she liked looking at him and thinking about the fact that she was to be his wife, but she nodded. She would need to start caring for Tommy as well, so that everything could go as Mr. Merriweather had asked.

Samuel got back up from the couch and rushed off to the staircase in the hall. The house had more bedrooms than she had expected based on how it looked from the outside. She wondered if Tommy's room would be close to hers should he need her.

A few minutes later, Samuel came down the stairs holding a small boy who wore a nightgown and clung to his father's shoulder. Samuel smiled and sat on the couch beside Abigail, with Tommy in his lap. "This is Tommy," he told her. "He is five years old and he is not feeling too well, but he is a sweet boy. Aren't you, Tommy?"

Tommy nodded timidly. He looked at Abigail and then averted his eyes. She smiled at him. He had his father's dark, curly hair. His eyes were gray like the sky before a storm. He would surely be handsome, should he make it to adulthood. She silently prayed that he would.

"It is wonderful to meet you, Tommy," Abigail said. "My name is Miss Copeland, but you can call me Abigail." She looked from him to Samuel. "You can call me Abigail too, if you like." She smiled at him. "Miss Copeland makes me feel like I've become my mother."

Samuel chuckled. "Then you may call me Samuel," he replied. "Or even Sam. The only people who call me Mr. Merriweather are my employees." He winked at Abigail and she sighed a bit. There was a certain friendly ease about him that she had not imagined him possessing. She had been expecting a solemn, serene widower. Perhaps this was his way of providing a more positive environment for his son?

Carefully, Abigail took Tommy into her lap. She listened to his breathing and noted that it seemed labored. "Has Tommy been to the hospital at all recently? How long has this been troubling him?"

Samuel's smile faded slightly. "He has been sick this way a little over a year. I take him to the hospital in town pretty regularly, for monitoring. They say he has asthma."

Abigail tutted softly. Asthma was a serious, chronic condition. She wondered if the young boy might have contracted it from being around coal mines in town. "If you don't mind my asking, how often do you go into your mines?"

Samuel shook his head. "Not as often as I used to. As the owner of Merriweather Mining Corp, I oversee the workers now, instead of going down into the mines on a daily basis."

She smiled slightly. "That's good. I don't want little Tommy to be around coal dust in the air, and I don't want you getting sick either." Abigail had only been there for a few hours, but she already cared about her new little family.

****

Tommy Merriweather had a breathing apparatus in his bedroom. Abigail looked at it as she settled him down in bed for a nap. It appeared to be such a harsh, robotic fixture in his room and it made her sad that the adorable little boy had to be tethered to such a contraption. Still, she was glad that it proved useful in helping him breathe while he slept.

Reaching down, she gently petted the dark curls on his head. "He never complains," Samuel said quietly, watching the two of them from the doorway of Tommy's room. "Even when his mother died, he simply cried and asked me what we should do. He is so good at accepting things for what they are and moving forward as best as he can...it must be something he got from Gertrude."

Abigail looked over at him and smiled. She joined him in the doorway. "You seem to have managed pretty well, too. If I may say so, sir." She blushed a little, hoping she was not being impertinent.

Sam smiled back at her and took her hand, squeezing it affectionately. "Of course you may," he said softly.

Helen Copeland came down the hallway and saw the pair holding hands. She smiled knowingly at Abigail. "Have I missed much?" she asked them pleasantly. "I took a short nap in my room in the hope of waking up for your arrival, Mr. Merriweather, but I seem to have been a bit delayed."

He chuckled softly, releasing his hold on Abigail's hand. He gave Helen a slight bow. "It is a pleasure to meet you, Mrs. Copeland. You have not missed much. Not much goes on in this house that one could 'miss'. I was just introducing Abigail here to my son."

Helen looked at him searchingly. His looks seemed to make her happy as well. Though looks were not everything, as she would be the first to tell Abigail. The key to a good husband was more in what he did, not how he looked whilst doing it. "I have heard about your little boy," she said softly. "I am sorry that he is not well, sir. I hope that our presence here will help to lift his spirits somewhat. And yours as well."

"I thank you for that," Sam said. "Now, please, may I request that you both join me for supper? I will find Bertha and make sure that it is ready as soon as possible."

Though he was young and a little bit nervous when it came to hosting his guests, Samuel was friendly and obviously doing his utmost to make sure that Abigail and Helen Copeland were comfortable.

He went off in search of his silent housekeeper as Abigail and her mother went into the home's dining room. They admired the fine linen of the table cloth. Abigail wondered how much influence the late Mrs. Merriweather had had on the home. It surely looked like it was in need of some sprucing up, but Samuel should be proud of how neat he had kept it.

The thought of 'sprucing up' the place reminded Abigail that one thing the home needed for the approaching holiday was a Christmas tree. She thought that a large, colorfully decorated tree would help to make Tommy feel better. What child did not enjoy the Christmas season?

Bertha soon joined the women in the dining room and asked them what they would like to eat for supper. She went off to prepare them a nice ham meal in the kitchens and Samuel returned, smiling and clapping his hands together once.

"I trust that you are both settled in here," he said politely, looking from Abigail to her mother. "Please, at any point, if you need anything, do let me or Bertha know. It has been a long time since we had guests – and even longer since we have had women around, other than Bertha, of course."

Abigail smiled gratefully at him. "There is one thing I was thinking about," she said shyly. "Since the Christmas season is nearly upon us, I was thinking that it would be nice to have a tree. It does not have to be a very large tree," she added, "just one that is big and grand enough, with decorations, for little Tommy to enjoy."

Samuel beamed at her. "I like the way you think," he said. "Tomorrow morning, I shall endeavor to go out into the woods and chop down the best looking tree I can find."

The trio sat down at the dinner table and Bertha brought in a glazed ham on a platter, served with potatoes and broccoli on the side. Abigail and Helen happily ate their meals, smiling at Bertha and Samuel. Abigail thanked her lucky stars that she had found such a kind, caring man to take her in and make her life better. She knew with no doubt that she was making Sam's life better, too, just by being there. She hoped that she would be able to bring comfort to Tommy's life and make sure that his asthma stayed under control at least, if she could not make it entirely go away.

"I am sorry that I did not meet you at the train station," Samuel said. "I had to run to the store to get some more medicine to sooth Tommy's coughing fits."

Abigail waved a hand at that. "Don't be sorry," she said kindly. "We believed that something like that must be the case. You have been caring for him by yourself for a long time. But now that we are here, you will be able to relax some."

Samuel smiled appreciatively at that. "You really are my angels. I'm so grateful to have you here. Thank you."

****

The next morning, Sam was true to his word. He went out bright and early before work and chopped down a tall spruce tree. Abigail awoke to the sound of him doing his best to quietly drag it into the house. He left it in the sitting room and went off to work at Merriweather Mining Corp.

Abigail padded down the stairs to have a look at the tree. It was propped up nicely against the wall, but she knew that they were going to need some kind of stand for it. She wondered if Samuel was good with woodwork and would be able to make a Christmas tree stand.

Quietly tiptoeing back upstairs, she went into Tommy's room. He was awake, looking up at the ceiling, breathing through his apparatus. "Good morning," Abigail softly said to him.

He looked over at her and smiled slightly, though the apparatus made it difficult for him to move his mouth much.

"Are you ready to come downstairs? Your daddy has a surprise for you."

She carefully unfastened him from his breathing aid and lifted him from his bed. As she carried him down the stairs, Tommy clung to her and her heart soared. He trusted her already, which made her so happy and relieved.

When they reached the bottom of the steps and he saw the tree in the sitting room, he got so excited that she had to set him down. He rushed over to the tree, happily jumping up and down like any other five year old boy. She smiled at him, hoping that the jumping would not aggravate his ailing lungs but glad to see him moving around like a healthy child. "It's perfect!" he declared. "When can we decorate it?"

He started to wheeze a little bit, so Abigail picked him up again and carried him over to the couch for some rest. Tommy continued to stare up at the tree in wonder as he calmed down.

"Your father is working hard so that we will all have a wonderful Christmas this year," she told him, carefully brushing his hair behind his ears.

Tommy looked up at her as she held him. "Are you going to be my new mother?" he asked her.

She felt a bit awkward discussing such things with the portrait of Tommy's late mother right there above them on the wall. Abigail had also not quite had the conversation with Samuel yet. It was assumed that they were to be married any day now, but she did not want to let Tommy know that in case Sam had not had the chance to explain the situation to his son.

"No one can be your 'new mother'," Abigail told Tommy in a hushed voice. She gazed up at the portrait of the beautiful, mysterious young woman who was Tommy's mother, and Samuel's wife. "Your mother will always be your mother," Abigail told the child. "And she will always be with you…I am here to take care of you and love you as much as I can, but I am not going to replace her in your heart. Do you understand?"

Tommy nodded slightly. He looked up at the portrait of his mother. "I miss her," he said sadly. "But I am glad that you are here with me now."

She smiled and cuddled him. "I am too," she said.

Samuel Merriweather came home to find his new little family all gathered around in the living room, working together to get the Christmas tree situated in the best spot. Even Bertha was there, helping to make sure that the tree was moved to suit Abigail and Tommy's specifications.

"We should not forget this," he told them with laughter in his voice. He went into the washroom and came out with a large vase full of water. Setting it down beneath the tree, he carefully lifted up the spruce and let it sit inside the vase. "This way, it will continue to stay looking green and lively," he said, winking at his son.

Since everyone was working together and seemed to be in the festive spirit, Samuel went off again and came back with a box full of Christmas decorations. Everyone worked together to hang ornaments and candles on the tree. At one point, he and Abigail attempted to put their ornaments on the same branch.

She blushed at him. "Go ahead," she told him.

He looked into her eyes. "No, you had it first."

Bashfully, she placed her bauble on the bough.

Samuel placed his ornament on a branch below hers, then he took her hand in his and gently squeezed it. "Abigail," he said, keeping his voice low so the other merry-makers would not overhear them. "Would you please do me the honor of becoming my wife this Christmas? T'would be the best gift you could bestow upon me."

She gazed into his gentle blue eyes as her stomach fluttered with excitement and feelings of love. Abigail had not known Samuel very long, but she could see that he was a sweet, loving man. How on earth could she turn him down?

She smiled and nodded. "Nothing would make me happier than to be your wife," she replied.

Beaming at her, he brought her hand to his lips and gave it a kiss.

Before too long, the Christmas tree was decorated. Bertha went off to prepare everyone a hearty lunch. Tommy, though still a bit wheezy, was showing signs of improvement from the way he had seemed to be before the Copelands' arrival.

As they all sat around the table, Abigail was so happy because it truly felt like they were a little family. She helped to cut up Tommy's sandwich into bite-sized pieces and made sure that he ate slow enough to not choke. His spirits had definitely been lifted by the Christmas tree. Perhaps that was not the only thing to have cheered him up…

****

The church where Abigail and Samuel were to be married was all done up for Christmas as well. There were green garlands and red ribbons all over the aisles between the pews. Abigail thought it was just about the prettiest thing she had ever seen. True to what Samuel had said, they were to be married on Christmas Eve and be each other's Christmas presents.

Several people from the little town of Coos Bay were there to witness their marriage. Abigail could tell that quite a few of them were Samuel's mining friends and employees. They seemed friendly, and hooted with joy as she walked down the aisle to meet Sam before the priest. She was wearing a lovely white lace dress that her mother Helen passed on to her from when she was married to the late Mr. Copeland.

Sam looked especially dapper in a gray suit and a dark blue tie. She mostly saw him in his mining attire, even though he did not mine so much anymore. It was thrilling to see him looking so sharp. He looked every bit the handsome prince of her dreams. He took her hands, gazing affectionately into her eyes. "My sweet Abigail," he said. "Before you came along, I was not sure what was to become of me and Tommy. Your gentle ways and loving heart have been a blessing to me. You're my gift from afar and I cannot wait to share a life with you here."

He leaned in and kissed her cheek before slowly placing her wedding ring on her finger.

The priest asked if she had anything to say. Abigail nodded, clearing her throat a little bit.

"I used to think that my life was pretty much planned out and settled for me, but something was missing. That something was you and little Tommy. I feel more at home here in this strange place than I could ever feel back in New York. I am so glad to have found you."

Abigail slowly placed the ring on Samuel's finger. Her hands were shaking a bit, but she was able to keep them steady enough to do their job. As soon as the ring was on him, she looked up into his eyes excitedly, biting her lip.

Once they were wed, Sam dipped Abigail back a bit and gave her a passionate kiss. She felt herself blushing and willed herself not to faint from how romantic it was.

A white horse and buggy brought the family home. Abigail felt as if she was in a fairy tale.

"Are you my new mother *now*?" Tommy asked her, drowsy and happy, as she carried him to bed for his nap.

"Do you want me to be?" she asked him, rocking him a bit in her hands to help prepare him for a good sleep before dinnertime.

He nodded. "Oh yes. Very much!"

She chuckled, laying him down in the bed and tucking the blankets around him so he would not get cold. "Then I am. But remember what I told you," she cautioned to him. "Keep your mother close in your heart, always. She will always be with you, watching over you and keeping you safe."

He put his little hand in hers and squeezed with as much energy as he could muster. "I will remember her. But you will keep me safe, too. I just know you will."

Abigail smiled down at Tommy. "You do?" she asked, feeling touched. "How do you know?"

Tommy smiled back at her, closing his eyes. "Because Daddy says you're an angel."

SOPHIE'S CHRISTMAS ON THE FRONTIER

Baltimore, Maryland - 1880

Sophie Miller loved life in Baltimore. She was a school teacher and had two children of her own: Theodore and Anna. In her group of single lady friends, she was the most outspoken against marriage, for she believed that working and creating her own success was better than depending on a husband. Her friends were amused by her independent spirit, especially because they knew she had not always been that way. She had been married to a fisherman prior to becoming a teacher, but her husband Alfred died in 1876. After a period of mourning, she decided that she must take things into her own hands and earn a living for herself and her small children.

That was, until her friends began to get married. One by one, they began to move away, seeking happy marriages out west instead of staying with her in Baltimore. Sophie went from feeling strengthened by her free spirit to feeling lonely. It was no longer a good thing, to be without a husband. All of her friends were off experiencing adventure in new places, and she started to feel the call to go west, too.

"After all," she reasoned. "The west must surely need teachers!" Sophie started to collect newspapers, reading carefully through all of the advertisements for mail order brides. There was something rather thrilling about the listings. She felt as though she was applying for a new position as opposed to seeking out a man. She hoped that these brave, interesting new men would allow her to retain her freedom.

One such advertisement made her both blush and laugh – surely a good sign. "Mister Randolph Parker, thirty two years old. Seattle. He is an honest, good-natured fellow seeking a beautiful, young bride who will honor him and laugh at his jokes," she read aloud to Teddy and Anna. They sat on her lap, looking over the ads with her, though being five and seven they could not make sense of them. "Owner of a logging company. Must love the outdoors and cooking over an open fire."

Sophie smiled. She had never cooked over an open fire, but she loved to cook meals for her children with their stove, so she was sure she could figure out how to do so over open flames. "What do you think?" she asked her children. "Does he sound nice?"

"What's a logger?" Teddy asked.

"A logger is someone who cuts down trees and turns them into things like this chair we are sitting on," Sophie answered. Gently, she set the children down on the floor. "Now you two run along and play while I write back to Mr. Parker, okay?"

They nodded and ran off to their play room, leaving her alone with her paper and her thoughts.

Dear Mr. Parker,

My name is Mrs. Sophie Miller. Your advertisement seeking a bride greatly amused me. I am a widow and I live in Baltimore with my two children, Theodore (Teddy) and Anna, ages seven and five. I am a teacher and I enjoy my job, but it has occurred to me that I should find someone to share my days and be a good companion to me and a good father for my children. I believe that you may be the person I am hoping for.

Please write back to me and let me know if my prediction is at all true. I love exploring the forests of Maryland and I imagine that Seattle must be extraordinary.

Yours sincerely,

Sophie Miller

She placed the letter in an envelope and chuckled at herself. Anticipation made her feel as though he would be able to respond to her much more rapidly than the pony express would allow. She had gone from not caring about another marriage to being excited by the idea. All it took was finding someone appealing in a strange, new world.

****

Sophie was often warning her students not to look out of the window during class. Now that she was awaiting a reply from Mr. Parker, she found that *she* was doing much of the window-gazing, dreamily imagining what life might await her across the country.

She hoped that she was beautiful and amiable enough for Mr. Parker's liking. He had not asked for any photographs, but she knew that a question about that must come at some point. Time only served to toy with her emotions, making her question herself and wonder if Mr. Parker would even respond to her. Did the men who posted advertisements get thousands of replies?

Finally, almost four weeks after she sent him a letter, she received a reply from Seattle. Sophie opened the envelope with some trepidation, praying that her letter had been well received.

Dear Mrs. Miller,

How joyous I was to receive your response to my advertisement. I had heard good things from some of my friends about the service, so it is a relief and a comfort to know that it was successful in leading you to me.

I was sorry to read about your late husband; however your children sound delightful. I am a widower myself, with a small daughter of my own. Her name is Gwen and she is also five. With any luck, she and your children will be fast friends.

Since my wife's death, Gwen has unfortunately been left rather lonely. I am very busy managing my logging business, and though she is under the care of a great governess, I do believe that given your skills as a teacher you would be a wonderful friend and tutor to her. I shall not dismiss her governess, of course, until we are sure that this would work out to our mutual satisfaction.

I am pleased that my advertisement amused you. I must admit that I have had some assistance with writing these letters – from Gwen's governess. I am well-spoken but not quite well-written, if you can understand.

If I have not completely changed your mind about me, I have also included some photographs of myself. I will look forward to your response, but will acknowledge that I may have frightened you away with my visage and my lack of wit. However, I shall hope against that.

Warm regards,
Randolph Parker

Sophie found herself smiling several times as she read the letter. She read it three times, feeling more excited each time. Then, she turned to the photographs that had indeed been enclosed in the envelope.

Mr. Randolph Parker had dark hair and a mustache. He was dressed well, in a handsome suit. In his hand, he held a bowler-type hat. He appeared much more well-to-do than she had been expecting, but that only made Sophie happy. He was clearly successful. She wondered how long he had been working in the lumber business. Perhaps he had even made a bunch of homes. Perhaps he could build a school for her...

****

The photographer that Sophie visited was highly professional. She could not stop admiring the photographs that had been taken of her. It had taken a long time to get them back, so she was relieved to see that she appeared quite lovely in them. Her long, auburn hair fell in curls against her shoulders in one of the portraits, and it was styled up in a bun in the other portrait. Her blue eyes stared out, ghostly and mysterious. She hoped that Mr. Parker would find her as lovely as she felt. It was rare that she had a professional take her photograph, but she believed this was a good occasion to do so. The older photographs that she had did not show how she appeared presently. She hoped that the extra bit of care she took would prove helpful in her flirtations via mail with Mr. Parker.

Sophie tucked the photographs into her envelope and wrote him a reply on some lightly-perfumed stationary.

My dear Mr. Parker,

A governess is a splendid way of seeing to little Gwen's education, as well as your own. Before I was married to the late Mr. Miller, I served as a governess to a wonderful family. I would enjoy serving as Gwen's tutor and perhaps her governess and myself could form a partnership to further along her schooling. It is my wish to establish a small school in Seattle, should that be acceptable, of course. I am unsure how many children live in your area, but I would love to teach whoever is around for the teaching.

Dear Mr. Parker, you are ever so silly. Your portraits were divine. You are both handsome and clearly well bred. In fact, I do believe that God has sent you to me. Right as I was beginning to believe no one was out there who could fill the void left by my poor Alfred, along you came. You are ever so amusing and ever so sweet. I pray that we shall meet each other and share a new, happy life and family together.

Yours fondly,
Sophie Miller

She read over her letter and placed it gently into the envelope. She wished that she could see his reactions to her notes. Would he appreciate her portraits as she had appreciated his? The pony express made her feel as though Seattle was now nestled beside Baltimore, yet she wished with all her heart that she could feel his hand is hers and know that he was truly there with her. She longed for him in a way that she had never longed for anything. Loneliness and a desire for Mr. Parker had crept up on her and now she no longer knew what to do with herself. She was twenty-eight years old, and yet she felt again the romantic youthfulness of a sixteen year old. Time was moving along so slowly, and it was now also moving backwards. When would her Romeo come for her? Could she dare to dream that their ending would be happy?

****

The mail carrier certainly seemed to enjoy making her wait. Sophie spent the next four weeks trying not to distress herself too much with how things might work out. She focused on teaching and taking care of her children, but her heart seemed to no longer be in the things she used to enjoy. Her mind often drifted away, thinking of places and people she had not even met, hoping that she soon would.

She received a letter postmarked from Seattle right as she was beginning to think she might never hear from Randolph again.

Dear Mrs. Miller,

I hope that this letter finds you and your children well. I have spoken with Gwen and her governess, and we all agree that you should come out here to Seattle and be with us for Christmas. It has been far too long since we have last had the company of family and friends. Gwen's mother was quite good at decorations and that sort of thing. Perhaps you are, too? You don't have to decide if you want to decorate a house you have not seen, however. Please simply consider the idea.

I can have some rooms prepared for you in my home, or I can make preparations for you at a nearby lodge if you think that would be more comfortable.

I have enclosed some boarding passes for you, Teddy and Anna on a ship that will sail from Baltimore to Seattle.

Looking forward to meeting you at last!

Warm regards,

Randolph Parker

Sophie nearly jumped for joy after reading his response. "Children!" she called. "Children, we are going to move to Seattle!"

Teddy and Anna ran into the room, holding hands like the good boy and girl they were. Sophie smiled proudly at them. "The nice man that I have been writing letters with has asked us to move to Seattle to be with him and his family."

"Is he the logger?" Teddy asked, scratching his scruffy brown hair.

Sophie laughed lightly and nodded. "Exactly. He is a nice man who works with trees to make houses. He wants us to be there for Christmas. Won't that be wonderful?"

Anna pouted a little. "But if we're there and not here, how will Santa Claus find us?"

"Aww," Sophie said, gently petting Anna's long, golden locks. "Santa Claus can find you. He knows where you are, always."

"He does?" Teddy asked, his eyes widening.

"Oh yes," Sophie said, sincerity coating her voice. "He watches you throughout the year; making plans to give you cheer." She gave them a little wink. Being a teacher meant that she had to employ some creativity at times, and that spread to her parenting skills.

Her children were both staring at her in awe. Christmas was not for several weeks, but she had certainly awakened their hopes. She felt incredibly hopeful and blessed. This transition to Seattle was going to be amazing, not just for her but for her children as well.

****

The ship ride started out being less than amazing for them. Sophia felt sick almost as soon as the boat began to rock, and Teddy seemed to become sick with panic at the idea of truly leaving the home he had always known. No amount of reassurance could help them calm down and she spent the entirety of their first night and day on the ship in their cabin with them, holding them and trying to convince them to sleep. Sophie began to fret that she and Alfred had not taken the kids out on the water enough. She loved the outdoors and being on sailboats, but her children had not quite acquired the skill and taste for it. She hoped that Mr. Parker would not be unhappy about that. Maybe little Gwen could introduce Teddy and Anna to boating. Sophie was not entirely sure that Gwen enjoyed boats. She did not know much about the child. What she had imagined was that Gwen was precocious and a bit lonely. Who knew what she might really be like?

This journey west was going to lead to so many magnificent things for the three of them; no, the whole new family of them! Sophie laughed a bit at herself, thinking about how she had been so set against having a new husband. Now, here she was, altering her home and everything with it to be with a man. A stranger, no less. As much as she admired and adored Mr. Parker, he was still a stranger that she would not fully know until she had spent some time with him. There was something exciting about it, however. She was truly excited to be meeting such a charming man with the possibility of becoming his wife! She would never have believed it a year ago.

Sitting in a chair on the desk of the ship, gazing out at the sun as it reflected on the waves, holding her sleeping children in her lap, Sophie looked forward to meeting Gwen and her father, the handsome and amusing Mr. Randolph Parker.

Seattle, Washington – 1880

One of the nice things about travelling to Seattle from Baltimore was that both cities were port towns, so boats could go straight to them. Sophie would not have liked having to board a train directly afterwards, as she had heard about from her friends when they had gone off to meet their prospective grooms. She felt no small satisfaction as she stepped off of the ship, holding each of her children by the hand. Seattle smelled like salt and fish, which was a familiar and enjoyable smell to her. "We're home," she told her children happily. "Isn't it wonderful?"

Teddy even smiled a little bit. "It smells like home."

Anna was very sleepy so Sophie picked her up as they went in search of their waiting carriage. A man followed with their luggage and helped to load it into the coach that came for them.

A door in the back seat of the carriage opened up and the young man from the photographs appeared. He grinned at Sophie. She smiled back at him and adjusted the sleeping Anna against her hip. "Mr. Parker," she said, a bit breathless from the surprise at seeing him so quickly. She did not know what she had expected, but she had not been imagining him waiting for them at the docks.

"Greetings, Mrs. Miller," he said in a friendly, happy tone. He held the carriage door open for her, Anna and Teddy. "I wanted to come and make sure that you arrived safely. I will not break from custom and sit with you. I'll sit in the front with Lawrence, my driver."

Sophie blushed and smiled at him, gratefully getting into the back seat of the carriage. She kept little Anna in her lap so the child would not be disturbed. "You are too kind," she told Mr. Parker. "Thank you."

They rode along in the carriage and Sophie looked out of the window with Teddy, pointing out the beautiful, tall trees that surrounded them. Those were surely trees that Mr. Parker used to make lumber. They must have been thousands of feet tall.

A light dusting of snow was on the ground. Perhaps they would enjoy a white Christmas in their new home. Sophie smiled, imagining the tall trees as Christmas trees, full of ornaments and light. What a beautiful place Seattle was. She thought she had known wilderness before, but this was like no other.

The carriage stopped outside of a large manor. It was made of wood, and the design had a welcoming, homelike feel to it. Sophie was tickled that this was to be her new home. She felt like a princess as Mr. Parker opened the carriage door for her and her children.

"Welcome to my home," he told them, smiling brightly.

Teddy stared up at him. It had been two years since he had had a father figure to look up to. Sophie hoped that they would become fast friends, but she did not want to pressure either of them.

Mr. Parker led them up the path to the front door and held it open for them all to pass through. Anna started to wake up and looked around at the inside of the house, bleary-eyed. "Is this home?" she asked.

Sophie laughed softly, a little embarrassed at the question. She looked at Mr. Parker and smiled. "We have been invited to live here," she said. "This is your home now."

Introductions would need to be made, but the children were too awestruck and exhausted to be as polite as Sophie wanted them to be.

"Mrs. Pierce?" Mr. Parker called before turning to Sophie and giving her a polite bow. "Please excuse me a moment." He went off into the recesses of the house to find the governess, Sophie assumed.

She took the opportunity to admire the architecture of the house. It had beautiful dark wood and emerald green accents. She wondered if Mr. Parker had designed it himself, or perhaps he had even built it.

Mr. Parker was a charming and pleasant host. Sophie dared to dream that he would be a loving husband and companion to her, and a caring, supportive father to Anna and Teddy.

****

Before too long, Mr. Parker reappeared with an older, finely dressed woman in tow. Sophie was sitting on the sofa with Anna asleep again in her lap and Teddy doing a bit against her shoulder. Mr. Parker smiled adoringly at them.

"Mrs. Miller, please allow me to introduce Mrs. Pierce," he said to Sophie, keeping his voice down so her children could continue to rest. "She is Gwen's governess and she has agreed to be your companion while you are here in the house with me."

Sophie gave Mrs. Pierce a friendly look. "Hello," she said. "It is so nice to meet you. These are my children, Anna and Teddy. They are exhausted from travelling. Might I show them to their bedroom?"

"Of course, Mrs. Miller," the kind woman said with a small smile. She quietly came over and brought Anna into her arms. Sophie stood and took Teddy by the hand to follow the nanny to the children's bedchamber.

Once each child was safely tucked into bed and given a kiss on the head, Sophie and Mrs. Pierce went back down to the living room where Mr. Parker was waiting for them.

"I have been assisting Gwen for almost three years now," Mrs. Pierce told her proudly. "She is taking a nap at the moment, but wait until you meet her. She is the most charming child." She smiled at Mr. Parker and then sat down on the sofa, taking up her knitting from a basket on the nearby table.

Mr. Parker gestured for Sophie to take a seat on one of the chairs. "Now that you are here, please call me Randolph, or even Randy," he told her.

Once upon a time, she had called her husband 'Alfie'. Sophie blushed as she smiled up at Mr. Parker. "Then you may call me Sophie. I was just admiring your house. It is truly beautiful. Did your company build it?"

Randy beamed at her. "Thank you. It started off as my own project, but my loggers did all of the final work on it. When I was younger and Gwen was but a baby, we lived in a much smaller house. As you can see, my company and I have come a long way."

She appreciated his pride in his work. It was well-deserved. "I noticed the trees as we were riding here. Have you really climbed up them?"

Randy chuckled and nodded. "One thing you really cannot be if you hope to have any success at being a lumberjack is afraid of heights." He winked at her, which made Sophie blush further.

"He has fallen before," Mrs. Pierce piped up, twirling her yarn over her fingers. "The stories he tells will make you fear for his life, but he has given it up, thank goodness."

Randy looked down, a little embarrassed. Sophie noticed that he was blushing, which only served to endear him to her further.

"I would not think of it as giving up," she said, hoping to cheer him up and show that she supported him. "I think it is impressive to go from being a lumberjack to owning your own logging company. It's especially marvelous that you have been able to build such wonderful things like this house."

Mrs. Pierce smiled then. "He and his workers have built many of the buildings in town," she added. "It is indeed an honor to go from climbing and cutting to being in charge of many employees. Forgive me for my remarks, sir. They were ill advised."

Randy shook his head, chuckling quietly. "Think nothing of it. You weren't wrong." He turned his attention back to Sophie. "Would you like to go out and look at the trees with me one of these days soon?" he asked her. "Mrs. Pierce could stay here and look after the children, or you could bring them along if you like. It has been a while since Gwen last saw the land, or played in the snow for that matter. We have had several dustings these past few weeks. I predict a beautiful holiday is in store for us. Almost as though God wanted to put on a show to welcome you here."

Sophie laughed lightly. "I do believe He was showing off his skills when he made this place. Seattle is absolutely beautiful. I would love to go out and see more of the land with you. We shall have to ask if the children would like to come along. It would be wonderful to spend some of our Christmas out among the…what are those trees called?" She enjoyed nature and believed forests to be breathtaking, but, not being an outdoorsman like Randy, she did not know the proper names of a great many things.

Randy smiled at her. "They are called redwoods," he answered, his voice taking on an air of excitement. "They are also known as Sequoias. Sophie, wait until you see just how tall they are when you stand up close to them."

Sophie smiled shyly. She could not wait to go on adventures with him.

****

"Mama! Mama!" Anna shouted from her bedroom later in the afternoon.

Sophie rushed up the stairs to find her sitting up in bed, looking confused and scared. "Aww, Anna. Did you have a bad dream?"

Anna shook her head quickly. "Where are we?"

"Is this the logger man's house?" Teddy asked from his bed. He was also sitting up, but he was more mystified than scared. Sophie was grateful that her older child was right there with Anna to help calm his little sister down.

Sophie sat on the edge of Anna's bed and petted her daughter's cheek a bit with her fingertips. Anna felt warm, but not hot as Sophie had started to fear. She did not want her children to be sick so soon after arriving at Mr. Parker's – Randy's – home. "Yes, we are at Mr. Parker's home now. Isn't it lovely and comfortable?"

"We're in Seattle?" Anna asked with wide eyes. She had been so sleepy as they travelled from the docks to the house. Sophie knew that the little girl had not been able to pay attention to much of their new life yet.

Sophie smiled at her children. "Why don't you come downstairs and see? Mr. Parker may even take you outside and show you his yard. There is some snow on the ground!"

At the word 'snow', the children threw off their blankets and came out of bed, hurrying down the stairs to see the house and the new people they were going to live with, and the snow!

Laughing, Sophie followed them down the stairs. "You'll have to forgive their inquisitiveness, Randolph," she said pleasantly, smiling when he came into her view. "They have never lived in a place like this, or seen such wondrous trees."

Anna and Teddy were staring out of one of the large windows, into the house's back yard. It was becoming dark outside as the sun set, but they could make out the white on the ground and the greenness that surrounded them.

"Children, come and meet Mr. Parker and Mrs. Pierce," Sophie called to them.

They turned from the window and came over to stand on either side of their mother. Anna clung to Sophie's skirt, sucking her thumb a bit in her nervousness.

Mrs. Pierce rose, smiling, from the couch and set her knitting aside. She joined Mr. Parker as he stood to meet the children.

"Randolph, Mrs. Pierce, these are my children, Anna and Theodore," Sophie introduced. She smiled down at the children by her sides. "Teddy, Anna, these are your new nanny and your… host." She blushed a bit. She did not quite know what she should have the children call Mr. Parker yet.

Randy, friendly as ever, grinned at Teddy and Anna. "You can call me Papa Randy, please," he said. Leaning down on his knees, he looked each of the children in the eye as he spoke to them. "I am glad to have you here with me for the holidays. Very glad. I hope that you will love it here."

Anna looked from him to her mother. "He is very nice, like you said, Mama."

Sophie smiled bashfully. She could feel that Randy was beaming at her, and he let out a warm laugh. "We were just discussing going out on an adventure tomorrow, to look at the evergreens and maybe pick one for our Christmas tree. What do you say to that?" he asked the children, keeping his eyes on Sophie, amused and happy at her blushing bashfulness. She definitely felt beautiful, when he gazed at her like that.

"Mrs. Pierce!" a tiny voice suddenly called from upstairs.

The governess smiled. "Gwendolyn! Excuse me a moment. The little miss of the house has awoken." She curtsied politely and rushed up the stairs.

Teddy and Anna looked at each other, surprised and happy to hear the sound of another child in the house.

"Will I be able to climb one of the trees, and cut it down like you do, Mr. Papa Randy?" Teddy asked, enthusiastic about the idea. Ever since Sophie had mentioned that Mr. Parker was a logger, he had been fascinated and wanted to learn all about it.

Randy laughed loudly at that, beaming proudly at the little boy. Sophie wondered if he was happy to get the chance to have a son now. "Perhaps someday you can become a lumberjack like me, but it will take lots of training before you shall be climbing any redwoods. Wait and see how tall they are. They are the size of a million of you."

Not to be discouraged, Teddy grinned back at him. "I can learn. I am a fast learner."

Randy gently put a hand on Teddy's shoulder. "I don't doubt that you are, my boy. I will be happy to show you."

Sophie bit her lip at that. She did not mind if Teddy was curious and wanted to help Randy with his woodworking, but she was not fond of the idea of little Ted going up into those tall trees. He could very possibly fall and break his little neck.

Anna was not paying attention to the boys and their logging talk, but she gasped and grinned when she saw Mrs. Pierce coming down the steps with Gwen.

Randolph Parker's little girl was as lovely as a porcelain doll. She had ringlets of strawberry blonde and eyes that were big, bright and blue, like her father's. It did not appear as though she had ever tampered with trees like her father, and Sophie could see that the girl had been well educated and trained in the proper etiquette of ladies.

All that Anna was concerned with was that Gwendolyn Parker was her age. She rushed up to the bottom of the staircase and smiled at her as Gwen hopped down to meet her. "Hello! My name is Anna Miller. We live here now. Your house is amazing and your daddy is nice and I am happy to meet you." She gave a little, excited curtsy.

Sophie was pleased to see that Anna remembered her manners, even if she was a little rushed because of her joy. "How do you do, Miss Gwen," she said. "This is my daughter. And this is my son, Theodore." She gestured an arm towards Teddy, who glanced over and smiled his hello.

Randy turned his attention to his daughter, and seemed overjoyed that Anna had already rushed over to her. "I think that you three are going to have such fun together," he said, smiling.

"I am pleased to meet you," Gwen said. She had the sweetest little voice. "Mrs. Pierce said we are going to pick out a Christmas tree."

Mr. Parker chuckled, rising up to his full height after his conversation with Teddy. "We won't go out tonight; it is much too dark and cold now. But we shall go out tomorrow morning, all right? Let's make a plan of it."

Gwen smiled. "That would be lovely," she said. She sounded like a little lady, which greatly amused and amazed Sophie. Mrs. Pierce had done a remarkable job helping to raise the girl. "May we have a very large tree this year?"

"Oh, the largest we can find, my dear," Randy replied.

The house had high ceilings, but Sophie did not believe they would be able to fit a whole redwood in the house. She was sure that Randolph could cut one into a suitable size, if they wanted, however. But surely there were trees that were smaller and more suited to their needs.

"I will help the cook get started with dinner," Mrs. Pierce offered. She went from the room, her skirts rustling against the hardwood floor.

"Come, Anna and Teddy," Gwen said, her voice sounding regal. "I will introduce you to my dolls." Carefully, she led them back up the stairs to her playroom.

Sophie was pleased that they were getting along so well already. She had not been too worried about it, but she knew that little children could find it difficult to be polite and generous with strangers. "Your daughter seems like she will be a great influence on my children," she told Randy, smiling at him.

"She gets that from her mother, not from me," he said modestly.

Sophie shook her head. "You have been a wonderful host for us thus far."

Randolph took her hand and gently kissed it. "So you do not regret your decision to come here and be with me? I felt for sure, once I saw those photographs and how beautiful you are, that you would change your opinion about me…"

She blushed, smiling at him. His words were flattering, but she believed he was being incredibly modest. "Oh, Mr. Parker, you are being silly again. You are handsome and you are a proper gentleman, just as I supposed when I read your letters and saw your photographs. Why, I do believe that we were made for each other. God works in mysterious ways, after all. I think perhaps He wanted us to find one another after losing…" She looked down.

Randy admired her dark, long lashes as she gazed downward. "Do not be sad, Sophie," he said sweetly. "I know what you mean. I believe it, too. I want nothing else this Christmas other than to call you my new wife."

She could not believe what she was hearing. It was not as if this trip was not planned with marriage in mind, but part of her had still thought of it more as a possibility, not a given thing. When she gazed up at Randy, he smiled at her and pulled a ring from his pocket.

"You've had that in your pocket this whole time?" she gasped, laughing a little and feeling overcome with emotion.

Gently, Randy placed the ring on her finger. It was gold, with a bright, sparkly diamond and a Celtic knot engraved on it. "This was my mother's ring," he told her. "She was Irish. I can get you another ring, if you don't like it."

Sophie beamed at him, tears slipping down her cheeks. "There you go, being silly again." She gave him a swift kiss on his cheek. "I love it. I shall be very proud to be your wife."

Randolph was clearly overjoyed. "I was so afraid that the advertisement would be ignored, or that the only response I would get would be from people who were laughing at me. It hasn't been easy, creating this home life we have now. I thought that, after Polly died, no one would want to be my companion and share in adventures with me."

"If we are being honest," Sophie replied, "for the longest time, I doubted that I would ever be happy with a husband again. I thought that I had everything I could ever want back in Baltimore. But then I read your note in the newspaper, and you made me smile and remember how nice it is to spend time with a man who truly cares for you."

Randy took her hand. "I do truly care for you," he said, smiling. "You and your children are a real gift to me. And to Gwen as well. She is already so happy to have you here with us."

He sat on the couch and she sat beside him, careful to keep a bit of distance between them. There would be plenty of time for cuddling once they were married. Sophie looked towards the fireplace hearth at the other end of the living room and imagined the sort of wonderful tree they would be placing there.

"I am going to be as excited as a child this Christmas," she told him. She looked down and saw that they were still holding hands. Blushing, she kept her hand in his, feeling comforted just by him being there for her.

****

The next morning, Randolph woke everyone up bright and early. Everyone dressed in their warmest clothes and put on coats. They were going out into the snow to find their Christmas tree. Sophie initially thought that they would be taking the carriage to his land of sprawling woods, but instead Randy led them out on a walk.

Thankfully, it was not quite as cold as it appeared when looking out the window. The snow was still a slight, dusty blanket on the grass. But it all was so beautiful! Sophie filled up with pride when she thought to herself that this was her home and this was her family.

Teddy bounded through the snow, pointing up excitedly at the tall Sequoias and Douglas firs. "Look at those!" he shouted to his sister. "Have you ever seen a tree so tall?"

Anna and Gwen were talking and giggling with each other. "Of course I have not," Anna told her brother. "You know I haven't."

Sophie walked along with Randolph and Mrs. Pierce. She could tell that Randy wanted to run ahead of everyone and be the tour guide, but he also clearly wanted to be close to Sophie. The calm, slightly dull governess did a good job acting as chaperone. Sometimes Sophie wished that the older woman would not tag along. Sophie was a grown woman who had been married before; surely she could handle time alone with Mr. Parker. But decorum prevailed.

The group finally came upon a gathering of pine trees that looked more like what Sophie was used to for Christmas. The gigantic trees dwarfed the pines, but that only served to endear them to her more. "Oh, how lovely," she said, her breath hanging in the air when she spoke.

"Do you want to do the honors of picking a tree, Sophie?" Randy asked, smiling at her.

She thought about it. "I think we should let the children choose," she said kindly. "As long as they are good and they don't argue about it." She knew that Gwen and Anna would behave, but Teddy might squabble a little bit. He was a young boy, after all, and he was the eldest and therefore more used to getting his way.

"Good idea," Randy said merrily. "Children! Stop here and take a look at these trees. We want you to work together and choose one to be our Christmas tree."

Teddy beamed, rushing over to the pines. He pointed to one. "I like the way this one smells!"

Gwen laughed. "I like the way this one looks. It matters more what the tree looks like, doesn't it?"

Anna sniffed a third tree, scratching her head a bit in confusion. "This one looks nice *and* smells nice," she concluded, looking over at Gwen and her brother.

Randy lumbered over towards them and admired the tree that Anna had picked out. He smiled. "This is a nice tree. It has lots of branches for ornaments." He turned towards Sophie. "What do you think?"

Rushing over, Teddy sniffed Anna's choice. He grinned and nodded. "It smells right and looks right," he said approvingly.

The tree looked perfect. Sophie gently touched one of its branches. "We have a winner," she said.

"Excellent!" Randolph shouted happily. "You all wait right here. I will go get my axe from our shed."

With that, he went off back through the trees towards his house. Sophie hugged herself to keep warm, though it still was a pleasant sort of chilly outside, not at all as frigid as she had expected. She smiled at Mrs. Pierce. "I bet Christmas is always beautiful here," she said to her.

The kind governess looked at her and gave a little smile of her own. "Now that you three are with us, I believe this Christmas will be the best one I have experienced at Parker Woods. You have no idea how lonely he and Gwen have been…"

Sophie was suddenly curious about what had become of Mrs. Pierce, but she did not want to ask for fear of upsetting the nanny. She realized that she and Mrs. Pierce had more in common than teaching.

"I am glad that you have been with them," she told her. "I imagine it's hard to find a good governess like you all the way out here."

Mrs. Pierce smiled a bit sadly. "My late husband used to work with Mr. Parker," she explained. "So I suppose you could say things worked out well, unfortunate though the circumstances were."

Sophie gently took the older woman's hand and gave it a squeeze. "You are part of the family," she said. "I am grateful to have you with us."

Just then, Randy reappeared with his axe. He had everyone stand back and chopped down the pretty-looking, good-smelling pine tree. Carefully, he lowered it to the ground and tied a rope around it for easier pulling.

The newly-formed family happily strolled along with him as he brought the tree back to the house. Everyone worked together to situate the tree in the corner of the living room by the hearth, where Sophie had anticipated it standing. Teddy filled a bucket with water and Randy carefully placed the tree inside it. They all then stood back and admired their work.

"Santa couldn't have found a better tree," Gwen said, and Anna blushed.

Mrs. Pierce took Sophie to one of the closets in the hall and they came back with a large box full of ornaments, garlands and wreaths. Randolph began leading them all in song as they decorated the tree together.

Hark! The herald angels sing, glory to the newborn king
Peace on Earth and mercy mild, God and sinners reconciled!

****

On Christmas Eve, carriages took the family to a nearby church. Everyone filed into the chapel and Teddy, Anna and Gwen sat beside Mrs. Pierce in the front pew. The church was done up splendidly with candles and green and white ribbons.

Sophie stood in her white wedding gown, feeling more nervous than she had felt when she married Albert. Or perhaps it was simply a different kind of nervous? When she walked down the aisle, she smiled up at Randolph and felt tears welling in her eyes. She never could have imagined, as she rode across the country to marry a stranger, that she would end up marrying a friend.

As she reached the altar, she was overcome with emotion as Randy took both of her hands in his. "Do you take this man to be your lawfully wedded husband," the priest asked her, "to have and to hold, to love and to cherish, to honor and obey, as long as you both shall live?"

Sophie blushed and nodded, tears sliding down her cheeks. She felt as if she was glowing and could float away at any minute. "I do," she said.

Teddy and Anna let out a cheer and she laughed a little. Randy grinned at her.

"Randolph," the priest said. "Do you take this woman as your lawfully wedded wife?"

Taking a cue from her, Randy nodded at Sophie before saying, "Yes, I do."

Her heart pounded throughout the rest of the ceremony, until at last the priest proclaimed that Randolph Parker could now kiss the bride.

Randy came forward a little and lifted her veil. Leaning in and caressing her cheeks with his strong and gentle hands, he kissed her mouth. She kissed him back, overjoyed to be Mrs. Parker at last.

Everyone was then asked to bow their heads as the priest concluded the ceremony with a verse from the Bible. "Love is patient, love is kind. It does not envy, it does not boast, it is not proud…"

When the new family arrived back at the house, the children all rushed to the windows to watch as it started to snow. Sophie admired how nice the tree looked, surrounded by children and snow coming down behind it. Randy went out into the back yard and returned a few moments later with arms full of logs for the fireplace. He started a fire going and sat in front of it with Sophie.

"You look absolutely beautiful, Mrs. Parker," he told her, gazing at her as she was lit up by the light cast from the fire.

"Why, thank you, Mr. Parker," she replied, smiling at him. "You are very handsome."

Randolph took her hand and kissed it.

Before long, the children begged to go sledding outside in the fresh snow. Mr. Parker chuckled and was quick to acquiesce, even though he would have happily stayed by the fire with his lovely new bride.

Sophie stood up. "I will go with you," she said. "Please allow me to change into something more appropriate."

Randy gave her one last look in her wedding gown before hugging her. "I love you," he said softly into her ear. Then he pulled back, admiring her with smiling eyes. "Let's go on an adventure!"

He entertained the children with stories about reindeer and snowmen while Sophie excused herself, going up to her bedroom to change into a warm, green dress. Since it was now snowing, she put on her thick coat and she decided to bring along a fur muff to keep her hands warm.

"Are you coming with us, Mrs. Pierce?" she brightly asked the nanny as she passed her in the hall.

Mrs. Pierce shook her head, though she smiled at her. "I will stay inside where it is warm. After all, today is your day." She went to her place on the couch and took up her knitting. Sophie went to her and hugged her around the shoulders.

"Thank you for all you have done."

Randy extended a hand to Sophie and she gracefully took it, going outside with the children to play in the snow and keep them from getting into too much mischief. Teddy pulled a sled around with the girls and sounds of shrieks and laughter filled the snowy air.

"What would you like this Christmas?" Randolph asked Sophie, holding her hand as they walked along, watching the children and admiring the thick blanket of snow as it formed and grew around them.

She gazed at him lovingly. "You mean besides being your wife?" she asked him pleasantly.

He chuckled. "Yes, besides that. Is there something else that would make you truly happy here?"

Sophie brought her hand back into her muff as she thought about her answer. "Well," she said. "I have been thinking that I would like to have a school here. It does not have to be fancy, but it could be someplace where I can teach the children… maybe even some other children in the town would like a school house. Mrs. Pierce could teach there with me. I can see that she is very skilled." She looked from him to Gwendolyn to prove her point.

Randy beamed at her. Sophie was relieved to see that her idea did not upset him. She of course would not let her work take her away from the home and being with him, but teaching made her happy and he had told her that he wanted to give her something that brought her happiness.

"You would like me to build you a school house?" he asked her, smiling widely. "I would be more than happy to. Why, we can design it together.

My men and I can get started on it right away."

She smiled and gave his cheek a kiss. "Thank you, Randy," she said. "I love you. What would you like me to give you for Christmas?"

He stopped walking and turned to face her, gently placing his hands on her shoulders. "You have already given me what I wanted," he said. "I am now the happiest man in Washington."

Sophie smiled and cuddled against him. "That makes me the happiest wife."

THANK YOU FOR READING!

If you enjoyed these stories, please visit
https://vlbrands.leadpages.co/hopemeadowpublishing
and sign up for our email newsletter, which includes updates on our FREE books, sales and new releases. Sign up today and get a **FREE** sweet historical romance ebook right now!

Warm Regards,
Hope Meadow Publishing

Printed in the USA
CPSIA information can be obtained
at www.ICGtesting.com
LVHW041005261024
794883LV00026B/277

9 781519 693976